Pride Publishing books by Matthew J. Metzger

Single Books
Best Behaviour
Enough

Starting Over
The Divorce
The Other Man

I0544691

Starting Over

THE DIVORCE

MATTHEW J. METZGER

The Divorce
ISBN # 978-1-913186-14-2
©Copyright Matthew J. Metzger 2019
Cover Art by Erin Dameron-Hill ©Copyright September 2019
Interior text design by Claire Siemaszkiewicz
Pride Publishing

Published in 2019 by Pride Publishing, United Kingdom.

Pride Publishing is an imprint of Totally Entwined Group Limited.

THE DIVORCE

Dedication

For Matti

Chapter One

"Tinder or Grindr?"

For a long minute, Aled's brain refused to understand the words. He stared blankly. He'd only been home for ten minutes and was still in his suit. Words like budget, memo, marketing directive—those words he could understand. Tinder and Grindr meant nothing.

"What?"

His best friend's boyfriend huffed an enormously annoyed sigh and Aled frowned.

"I don't usually get people knocking on the door asking about dating apps," he said defensively. "Not even you're that weird."

Tom just rolled his eyes. "Tinder"—he wiggled the phone in his left hand—"or Grindr?" He wiggled the phone in his right.

"Why do you have Grindr?" Aled asked slowly, then backtracked. "Why are you on my doorstep asking me about hook-up sites? With two phones? Who needs two phones? Why are you even *here?*"

"Er, fourth of January? You, me, Suze, drinks at The Mason's Arms? Any of this ringing any bells?"

"Not in the mood? Don't feel like celebrating? Thirty-three isn't an important number? Any of *that* ringing any bells?" Aled asked sarcastically and closed the front door.

Or tried to. Tom shoved his size twelve boot in the way and impeded matters somewhat.

"Tom, seriously, I don't feel like —"

"Tough," Tom said. "It's your birthday and we're not having no for an answer this time. And Suze is too soft to say no to you, so she sent me."

Typical.

"I don't want anything except a pizza in front of the telly. Now go away."

Tom snorted. "Is there someone sharing your pizza?"

"What? No."

"Then find one — Tinder or Grindr?"

"You're not going to leave, are you?" Aled asked, pointedly eyeing Tom's boot.

"No."

"Fine. I'll get my bloody coat. And put those phones away. *Why* do you have Grindr?"

Tom made an excuse about a spare phone borrowed from his younger brother and shoved his way into the hall. He even followed Aled upstairs to keep chatting outside his bedroom door while Aled found some jeans and a decent shirt. Aled tuned him out. Tom was a talker and always had been.

"That'll do," Tom said when Aled re-emerged. "Put the good coat on. We're going to get you laid."

Aled narrowed his eyes. "No chance. One drink. That's it. I don't feel like going out in the first place."

Tom stopped dead at the top of the stairs. He was a big lad, built for rugby and about as fluid as a brick wall. Aled, at five seven, had no choice but to wait for him to move.

"You haven't felt like doing anything for a year."

Aled's temper sparked. "That's none of your—"

"Knock it off," Tom said sharply. His usually jovial voice had dropped to a grave timbre. "It's been a year and all you've done is work mad hours. And when you do come home, you drink yourself into a stupor and go through all your pictures. Enough's enough. You've got to stop wallowing and start living again."

"She's my *wife*—"

"And she's gone."

Aled swallowed thickly, shaking his head.

"She's gone, mate. She's not dead—she left. She's moved on. Time for you to do the same."

The words were soft, but they felt sharp. Aled's heart tightened and he jumped when Tom's heavy hand landed on his shoulder and squeezed.

"Come on," he coaxed. "Come out for a few pints and a curry with me and Suze. Like we used to. If you don't want to hook up with someone, then fine. But let's have a laugh and go through some profiles anyway, yeah?"

Aled laughed bitterly. "You call that moving on?"

"I call it better than sitting here in the dark with your wedding photos."

"She's my wife. What else am I supposed to do? I love her. I still love her. I'm always going to love her."

"I know. And I'm not arguing with that. But you're heading right for a breakdown, mate, and you're a better man than that. You think me and Suze are just going to watch you chuck in the towel for Melissa?"

Aled blinked, startled. "Chuck in the — I'm not bloody suicidal."

"Don't have to be to train-wreck your life."

Aled worked his jaw but said nothing. Christ, no wonder Suze had sent Tom round if that was what they thought. The anger ebbed and was replaced with a sickly sort of guilt. He didn't see nearly enough of either of them these days — no pub quiz, no pint and pie on Friday evenings, not even swimming with Suze after work. He never left on time. Or he just didn't feel like it.

Tom was right.

He hadn't felt like doing much of anything.

"So your solution is to find me another wife?" he joked weakly.

Tom snorted with laughter and finally moved. The stairs creaked under their combined weight and he threw Aled's leather jacket at him from the hooks in the hall.

"I'm not talking love, you daft berk. No fucker finds love on Tinder and Grindr. I'm talking about sex."

Stooping to lace his boots, Aled laughed. "You what?"

"Sex? You know, clothes off, penis in vagina? Or in arse, whatever takes your fancy."

"You think having a shag will snap me out of it?"

"Might remind you there's better things to do than sit around waiting for things to change," Tom said flatly. "Might kick-start a bit of the bloody fun meter that's been sorely lacking lately. And I've got a couple of suggestions."

Aled smirked. "No offence, but we're not exactly into the same things."

"Understatement of the century, you kinky, queer bastard." Tom grinned then towed Aled out of the door and barely let him lock up. They walked to the main road in a companionable silence, then Tom hailed a taxi and told Aled to shut up and put up when he moaned about going farther than the local round the corner.

"Suze gave you plenty of chances to pick a place."

Aled grimaced. "I've got some making up to do, don't I?"

"No shit, Sherlock."

They talked Suze—Tom's girlfriend, Aled's best friend—and some new yoga class she was trying to get Tom involved in. Aled's throat felt rusty and his jaw ached, like he hadn't just *chatted* for an age. But his shoulders eased and the vague headache he'd been nursing all day at the office dissipated in Tom's relaxed company.

So when they got to the pub, Aled held up a credit card between finger and thumb and offered to get the first couple of drinks in.

"Not going to catch me arguing," Tom agreed.

When he came back from the bar, both phones were on the table. Tom was tapping out a text to Suze on his personal mobile, but Grindr was still open on his other one and Aled raised his eyebrows.

"Better not let her catch you with that."

"She uses it," Tom said. "Likes to check out the competition."

"*What* competition? They're all gay on there."

"Fine by me!" he said cheerfully. "She's on her way. Game of pool before she shows up and thrashes us both?"

"Yeah, okay."

Aled liked Tom. It had been a bit of an unusual change—Suze's taste in boys all through school had been god-awful and Aled had been almost on an autopilot of immediately hating her boyfriends just because they were the type of shit boy that Suze had fancied back then. But then she'd met Tom and everything had turned around. Tom was just…nice. Laid-back. Genial. Well-meaning. Had a habit of putting his foot in it right up to his backside, but he never meant anything by it. He was easy company and—despite his sharp tone at the house—rarely got involved in other people's business. If Tom wanted to play pool, they'd just play pool. They'd not talk or go hunting on dating apps. They'd just play.

They had a few frames in the quiet, pre-piss-up half-hour before the pub started to fill, and moved on to a better drinking hole when it got too busy. The night was cold, the pubs were warm and Aled slowly relaxed as the lager eased into his system. Tom had a point. This *was* better than sitting at home, mourning Melissa.

Suze joined them after the fourth pint, a flurry of platinum-blonde hair and kisses, shrieking "Happy birthday!" so loudly that half the pub started singing and Aled grumpily downed his fifth pint with the savage urge to make it all go away. At the same time, though, he did feel a bit guilty. Suze had been his best friend for thirty years, ever since they'd both attended the same nursery. He'd even married her when they were five, playing dress-up in his parents' back garden. He was an only child, but it had never felt like it with Suze there all the time. She had always been on his side, throughout everything—and there'd been a lot of everything throughout their collective sixty-six years—

and Tom's blunt words in the hall had jarred Aled a little.

He'd neglected her. In a year of wallowing with his photographs and empty house, Aled had forgotten to lean on her the way he always had. So after necking the pint, he leaned sideways and hugged her on a whim.

"Aw, sweetie, is Tom getting you plastered?" she enthused and kissed his cheek. "Good, you need a celebration. Thirty-three!"

"Don't remind me," Aled grumbled.

"Thirty-three and breaking a dry spell," Tom said, beaming. He had a huge grin that could swallow his whole face and Aled narrowed his eyes at it, sensing further traps.

"Breaking a dry spell?" Suze asked.

"*Your* boyfriend," Aled said, taking care not to start slurring, "is on Grindr."

"Your boyfriend has a brother on Grindr," Tom corrected.

"Mm, I'm sure it's *just* Daz," Suze said suspiciously. "Why are you on Grindr? And why does Aled know you're on Grindr?"

"Because it's hilarious, and because I told him," Tom said promptly and slid the phones across the table again. "So, Aled? Made your choice?"

Aled shrugged, draining the pint glass. "Fuck it, whatever."

"Grindr," Tom decided. "Women have screwed you around too much already."

"Excuse me! *This* woman has been amazing for him!"

"You're not shagging him, though."

"Is this what this is about?"

Aled left them to their minor domestic, dragging himself up to go to the bar and rubbing a hand over his face whilst waiting to be served. In truth, he didn't want to bother with any of it. But if letting Tom make him an account on Grindr and showing a bit of paltry interest would get them off his back, Aled would do it. He didn't *want* to sleep with anyone. He'd not so much as wanked since Melissa had left him, all interest killed by — by —

He blinked at the bar.

Fuck.

A year without so much as a wank? His whole marriage, they'd screwed two or three times a week. He'd lost his virginity when he was thirteen. Hell, he and Melissa had had an open marriage purely *because* they both had such high sex drives.

And yet he'd not so much as had a quick one off the wrist in a *year?*

Christ, maybe Tom was right. Maybe he *was* heading for a self-destruct.

"Another round, mate?"

"Yeah, yeah, thanks…"

"On the house. Heard the yelling it's your birthday and all. How young?"

Aled blinked. The barman was grinning at him, all gap teeth and eyebrow piercings. "Thirty-three," he said and the man guffawed.

"I bloody wish! Thirty-three, Christ, still got your life ahead of you! What you doing drinking it away in 'ere?"

Aled tuned out the cheery chatter, frowning at the bar. The guy was right. He was only thirty-three. And maybe if he did what Tom said, jump-started everything out of this rut, then he would get the impetus and the drive back to go after Melissa and talk to her about it properly. Maybe that was all she'd wanted, him to chase after her, like he had when they were teenagers.

He collected the round and lurched back to the table, banging them down, and said, "Right. Laid. Let's do it."

"No thanks, mate, you're a bit too furry for me," Tom quipped, but was grinning and tapping away. "Just setting you up now. Tell you what, I'll text Daz. He was going on and on about this guy he hooked up with when he was over, caused a right domestic, do you remember, Suze?"

"Oh, the repeat offender?"

Tom laughed. Aled frowned. "You what?"

"Yeah, Ryan said the guy was a repeat offender. Daz shagged him about four times, I think. Said he was brilliant. And Ryan didn't like that and they had a right barney about it. I'll text Daz and ask what he was called, see if he's still got his number or something. Sounds like just what you need."

"Not a *literal* repeat offender, I hope," Suze said snottily, then seized Aled's elbow. "You know what we need to do? Lose this dead weight and go clubbing again."

"Thirty-three, Suze. Not twenty-three."

"Thirty-three and doing good!"

"Thirty-three and getting fat," Aled corrected. "If I get my top off in a club like I did at your twenty-first, people'll be sick."

"With jealousy that you're not interested in them!" Suze sang, as Tom pushed the phone across the table.

"There. Start hunting."

Aled rolled his eyes and tentatively flicked through the offerings. Of which there were a *lot.* Seemed like West Yorkshire was a hive of guys who liked a bit of dick in their lives. But it was a bit depressing, too. Profile after profile detailing sexual positions, measurements, deciding that kinky meant the odd plug and a bit of whipped cream—Aled wanted to laugh. These people weren't kinky. They were just young, horny and thought vanilla meant the missionary position through a hole in the sheets. What the hell was he supposed to say to any of them? *Do* with any of them? They'd look at him and just see a thirty-three-year-old ginger shortarse with glasses, and assume he was as harmless and boring as he looked.

The phone buzzed, Daz's name flashing up along with the first four words of a message, and Aled pushed it back to Tom with an outstretched finger. "Text for you."

Tom buried himself in some frantic texting and Aled sat back, nursing his pint and scowling at it. Maybe he needed to get back into the scene. Or into it in the first place—he and Melissa had never really been into the actual BDSM scene. They'd more or less figured out what they liked on their own, but if Aled could…well, *borrow* someone for a bit, maybe, scout out a few other dominant types in the area and make use of a couple of their subs, perhaps.

"Oh, fuck me," Tom said and whistled. "Mate, *I'd* go gay for this one."

He pushed the phone back to Aled and a face stared up at him. Some summer snap, just a casual photo, sunglasses propped up on ink-black hair and even darker eyes almost smirking up at him. But it was the smile that got Aled's attention—perfect lips, flushed like he'd been giving head not five minutes before the picture was taken. He was shockingly attractive, so good-looking that Aled suspected it might be faked, or a photo of some random model, but —

God, that *mouth*.

His cock stirred, for the first time in a year, and Aled swallowed.

"Nice, right?" Tom said, grinning.

"Nice," Aled agreed, "but he's hardly going to want to go for someone like me."

"Daz is an ugly fucker and he banged him four times. Says he's sex mad. Just tell him you'll fuck his brains out and he'll probably pop right down here and join us," Tom said, grinning broadly.

angel23.

"What's his name?"

"Dunno, Daz didn't say. Says he's hot as fuck and a great shag, though. Leeds lad. Message him!"

Aled scanned the description. It wasn't much unlike the others — he bottomed, he wasn't interested in relationships, he —

What the —

I'm trans. Got a V and an A. Feel free to try either, or both if you're that good ;)

"He's trans," Aled said.

"You what?" Suze said, leaning over to look.

"He's transgender."

"What, he wants to be a girl?"

"Other way around," Aled said.

"Huh, maybe I wouldn't have to go gay for him..." Tom said thoughtfully and Suze smacked him. "Ow! What?"

"You're being an arse," she said loftily.

Aled hesitated, then opened a message tab. Why not? He'd done men and women. *angel23* couldn't have anything Aled hadn't seen before and he was fucking gorgeous, whatever he was packing. And that mouth would definitely help rattle Aled right out of this rut.

I'm that good, he sent. *Want to let me prove it?*

Chapter Two

Can I do your pussy then?

Delete.

What're you doing on here if you're a bird?

Definitely delete.

U do anal?

"Learn to read." Delete.

Wanna swap BJs?

"Not after the last time. Bye-bye." Delete.

I'm that good. Want to let me prove it?

"Oh, hello."

A newcomer. Gabriel smiled. He had a fair few regulars, like failed blowjob guy, but he was always interested in new people. The pool of fuckable guys who were up for a bit of fun with him could be depressingly shallow.

Newcomer didn't have many details. Just a blurry shot of some white guy in a pub. Drunk bet with friends, maybe, or a shiny new wannabe queer who was married to a blissfully ignorant wife. Gabriel didn't much care. He liked dick. Who cared what backstory was attached to it?

More disappointingly, the profile was bare bones. Gabriel wasn't exactly the fussiest guy on the planet, but he was an exclusive recipient. And in his experience, people named *gingerbiscuit* weren't going to be ramming it in there until it shook a tooth loose. He should pass, at least until some detail was forthcoming.

Still —

He'd had his shot last week. And that always made him antsy. The fortnight after a T day was like a sex paradise, presuming he could get it, and a puritanical hell if he couldn't. His blood had been thrumming for two days and wanking just wasn't doing the trick. He needed a fuck. A good, solid, hard fuck.

Only Kevin was still on holiday with the wife and kids, and Michael was being an arsehole lately and didn't deserve to stick his dick anywhere.

angel23: Dinner? V for starter, A for main course and if you're that good, I'll suck you off for dessert.

Gabriel tossed the phone onto the bed and swung his feet to the floor. The flat was chilly, which was probably why he'd woken up so early. He didn't have to go to work until midday.

The shower was hot and fucking his own fingers dissatisfying. He preened in the mirror for a little while, wondering if he ought to try a club without Kevin, but dismissed it as a dumb idea. Kevin would only find out, then he'd *really* beat Gabriel's arse. And not in the fun way. It wouldn't be worth it.

He heard the phone beep as he stepped out and drip-dried his way back to the crumpled bed. Grinning, he swiped it open. Newcomer was awake.

gingerbiscuit: I'm good enough you'll be begging to suck me off.

And promising.

"Nice," Gabriel murmured, thumbing quickly back to the fuzzy picture. He squinted. Light hair. Maybe the name was a hint. And glasses. Ginger guy with glasses and a point to prove, perhaps? Well, Gabriel would take that bet. Inferiority complexes always made for a good, savage fuck.

Still, not many guys knew how to fuck front *and* back and still have enough stamina left for a blowjob. Gabriel could count on one hand the number of men he'd fucked who knew how to have sex without inserting a penis somewhere, and Gabriel had shagged a lot more than a handful of men.

angel23: Quite possibly ;) But maybe after two courses, you'll be begging me not to?

gingerbiscuit: I don't beg.

"Oh, thank you, God," Gabriel whispered. Dominant. Top. Whatever the ginger guy liked to call himself, that was what he was. Short man syndrome or something like it, who the fuck cared? He was arrogant, which meant he'd be sexy and probably inconsiderate about getting inside. And Gabriel loved the sting of a harsh one.

Kevin always laughed at him and called him undomesticated. Jim, the closest Gabriel had ever had to a proper boyfriend, used to say he was wired up weird. But Gabriel had never really cared. He didn't like it gentle and slow and *boring*. He liked it rough. He liked handprints and walking funny in the morning. If he couldn't feel the fuck all the way from his scalp to the soles of his feet, then what was the point in having one in the first place?

And Gabriel would quite happily beg for it.

angel23: I do ;)

He usually played it a little cool with newcomers. Sexts and details. Testing out the solicited dick pics and screening for creeper vibes. But he chewed on a ragged edge of thumbnail, feeling the heavy pulse in his crotch. No Kevin. No Michael. And an arrogant ginger guy who refused to beg sitting in his inbox.

angel23: Are you free today, or do I have to beg for that too?

Fuck it. Gabriel needed it. He'd been fucked in public toilets before, no big deal. Unless the guy had a thing about sex in police cells or up telegraph poles, Gabriel had almost certainly been boned in weirder places than wherever was suitable to meet *gingerbiscuit*.

gingerbiscuit: I could make some time for you this morning. Whereabouts in Leeds?

angel23: Belle Isle.

He usually didn't bring newcomers to the flat. Glancing around his bedroom, Gabriel decided he'd best leave himself the option. There weren't many fuckable spots in Belle Isle that he'd want to be dropping his jeans in. Not a great place to advertise the possession of a pussy.

gingerbiscuit: Ten o'clock? Coffee, then back to your place? Via an alleyway if you look like your picture.

Deal. Gabriel darted back into the bathroom for the linen cupboard wedged between the shower and the door by some stupid architect way back when. Fresh sheets and a couple of clean towels. Thank God he always kept a spare set, if only because Jim had been a neat freak about bedsheets and left him in the habit.

Despite having lived alone for good few years now, Gabriel kept a tidy existence. Partly so he didn't have to clean much in case of unexpected company, partly because domestic servitude was one of Kevin's preferred uses for him on the rare occasion he came over. It didn't really get Gabriel off, but Kevin's monster cock could do that all on his own, so he tended to comply. And a sink-side fuck was good incentive to keep up with the dishes.

The flat was small and it didn't take him more than twenty minutes to spruce it up enough to be acceptable. He scouted out all the toys and shoved them in a drawer, though. First fucks were not to be allowed near handcuffs. Sometimes short-man syndrome took edgy angst a little bit too far.

Sweep-up done, Gabriel retrieved his phone and flopped backwards onto the sofa, still naked as the day he was born and with no intention of putting on underwear anytime soon. Being dry helped with the hurt — and the electricity in Gabriel's nerves *demanded* some hurt.

angel23: Coffee, two alleyways, my flat ;) Upload a better picture — it's not so dark at my place.

He waited for the expected dick pic, tapping his fingers hopefully against the back of the phone. Gabriel wasn't a size queen. He wasn't deep enough to need it and there was a distinct truth in everything being about how it was used. But it was nice to have a bit of an idea about what he was in for. Anticipation heightening the tension and all that.

To his surprise, Biscuit didn't offer one. Instead, he sent a name.

gingerbiscuit: The name's Aled. And you are?

Gabriel blinked. And you are? On Grindr? Without a dick pic?

What kind of a question was *that*?

Instantly, Gabriel upgraded his opinion. He wasn't just going to get fucked by an arrogant ginger later — he was going to get fucked by a posh boy. *And you are?* Posh boy, or fancied himself like one. Gabriel grinned, dropping a hand to touch himself lightly. Maybe Biscuit — no, Aled — maybe Aled would wear a suit. Be proper fancy. Gabriel had a bit of a thing for suits, but

Kevin never indulged it and Michael would look utterly ridiculous in one. Maybe Aled would come in one. In every sense of the word.

Slowly, he began to rub.

Getting down on his knees for some posh ginger lad in a suit? Lawyer-on-a-lunch-break-type scenario? Or maybe Gabriel was the defendant and couldn't afford the legal fees —

He scolded himself mentally and tucked the fantasy away in the back of his head. No kinky games near the newcomers. It only ever led to trouble.

But still —

And you are?

Gabriel grinned.

Best way to keep an arrogant posh boy interested was to keep him hanging.

angel23: Meeting you at ten.

Chapter Three

Aled woke up with a raging hangover, a mouth tasting like curry sauce and cushions, and a cat sitting on his neck.

Which meant he was on Suze's sofa.

"Gerroff, Meowth," he mumbled, swatting, but Meowth simply purred into his ear and didn't move. "Fuck's *sake*."

Undoing the becoming-one-with-the-sofa trick he'd performed somewhere around four in the morning was a delicate process, particularly not wrenching his shoulder or being sick in the middle of it, but once he was up, and Meowth had relocated to his lap like a normal cat, Aled felt more decent than he had any right to feel after eleven pints and a dodgy kebab.

Rubbing the back of his neck and slowly working the pain out of his shoulders, Aled peered at the living room with hungover eyes and grimaced. God, he'd not done this in a while and now he was remembering why. The pictures. *Everywhere*, the pictures.

Suze fancied herself a photographer and it showed. Every surface had a framed photograph—and Aled wouldn't have minded if they hadn't been the couple-y type of photographs associated with newly-weds. Pictures of her and Tom everywhere—on holiday, at his sister's wedding, on a random plane, in a sushi bar for her birthday last year, sitting on the bonnet of Tom's car…

Aled's gut twisted.

He used to have pictures like that.

He'd taken most of them down because it hurt too much to see himself and Melissa beaming at him from every wall, reminding him what he'd fucked up and lost. But then he kept opening the drawer where he'd put them to have another look, because it also hurt to *not* see them anymore. And it hurt to come to Suze's flat, to see her life with Tom on the walls and know he'd had that and lost it.

Fuck, he'd not even lost it. He'd driven it away.

Scrubbing both hands over his face, Aled took a shaky breath. He needed to go home. Last night had been a good distraction, and maybe he did need to work at moving on a little bit—or getting Melissa back—but sitting in Suze's living room staring at her couple-y photos with Tom wasn't going to help in the slightest.

He staggered up off the sofa, dislodging Meowth, and headed for the bathroom.

Suze's shower was hot and Aled stood under it for the longest time, clawing back his thoughts from his hangover. He borrowed Tom's toothbrush and gargled an obscene amount of mouthwash before re-dressing and scouting out the kitchen. There, he found his phone, discarded and covered in messages. Several were from Suze herself, obviously as drunk as he'd been, a happy birthday from Nana that he must have missed last night, one from Tom when Aled had staggered off to the gents telling him to hurry up and get back, one from Sky telling him his direct debit would be coming out of his account in three days, and —

Aled paused.

One on Grindr.

He clicked.

angel23: Dinner? V for starter, A for main course and if you're that good, I'll suck you off for dessert.

What the — ?

Aled blinked, genuinely surprised that *angel23* had replied to him at all, never mind in the positive, and he fumbled for a split second before the dominant in him stirred, roused — finally — by the prospect of sex.

gingerbiscuit: I'm good enough you'll be begging to suck me off.

What the hell was he doing? He wasn't *seriously* going to —

angel23: Quite possibly ;) But maybe after two courses, you'll be begging me not to?

So *angel23* was awake. Aled bit his lip, glancing at the holiday snaps on the fridge door. Could he just — go? Just do exactly what Tom had told him to do? Walk out, hook up and walk away again?

gingerbiscuit: I don't beg.

angel23: I do ;)

Aled swallowed. Christ. The guy was forward. And hitting Aled's buttons. Before he could think of something to say, though, *angel23* beat him to it.

angel23: Are you free today, or do I have to beg for that too?

Aled blew out his cheeks.

gingerbiscuit: I could make some time for you this morning. Whereabouts in Leeds?

angel23: Belle Isle.

A quick Google search found a Costa in south Leeds, and Aled sent the maps link, followed by, *Ten o'clock? Coffee, then back to your place? Via an alleyway if you look like your picture.*

angel23: Coffee, two alleyways, my flat ;) Upload a better picture – it's not so dark at my place.

Aled chuckled and took a quick selfie, sending it before adding, *The name's Aled. And you are?*

angel23: Meeting you at ten.

Aled smirked, left Suze a note that he'd gone home and thanks for the toothbrush, and let himself out. Change of clothes, condom then up to Leeds.

Fuck, he'd have to buy condoms.

It had been a while, but a man didn't forget that kind of detail. He stopped off at the chemist's in town to buy a packet and a bottle of lube for good measure. He had no idea if trans men could get pregnant, or if they went all dry in the front and would need a bit of help getting comfortable. In a way, he hoped so. Playing with someone to get them ready was just as good as the real deal, in Aled's opinion. Once upon a time, he'd been very good at sex.

Time to see if a year out of the game had changed anything.

It was early, so he took his time. Home for a shower and a change of clothes, then out again, keys and wallet in his jacket and condoms in his jeans. Belle Isle was not exactly a salubrious part of Leeds – in fact, Aled would say it was a shithole, to the point that he took the bus, rather than risk his car on some scabby street corner there. It was exactly where he expected some sex maniac from Grindr to live, truth be told. Perhaps *angel23* was even a professional whore, but Aled would be damned if he was going to pay for this. He wasn't *that* desperate.

The shop itself was actually quite nice and Aled parked himself in a chair by the window that stared down the main road, watching buses trundle past and a couple of blokes dealing drugs out of a car to passers-by, scarpering when a siren wailed somewhere in the estate behind them. Aled watched it all dispassionately and waited.

He knew he was being a bit harsh. Melissa had been from Eastmoor, the dodgiest part of Wakefield, and her family had been lovely. If Daz rated *angel23* so highly, he was probably nice enough. And Aled had been a student in Leeds. He'd lived in a flat that had been burgled eight times in one year and yet all his neighbours had been friendly little old people who used to call him and Melissa sweet. Two or three of them had come to the wedding, actually.

But still, he'd not go back. He didn't live in the nicest estate now, but at least he could park his car on the drive at night and still have four tyres when he came back out in the morning. He could leave his kitchen window open and not come downstairs to find a smackhead in his hall. He'd never been burgled there. Here, it was all too likely to happen.

So what was he *doing*, watching Belle Isle for some guy who wouldn't look like his picture and was offering to beg to suck Aled's cock?

Well, that was it right there.

He'd offered to beg.

Aled was no formal dominant, no tried-and-tested member of some community or club, but he *was* dominant. He had fantasies. He got off to violent porn — he got off to his partner begging him for what they wanted or begging him to stop doing what *he* wanted. It caused him issues, sometimes — a lot of them, actually, because Aled wasn't exactly comfortable with the fact that sex was a lot hotter if he was threatening his partner throughout — but it was the way he seemed to be wired. Melissa had been wired the other way and that had worked beautifully.

And *angel23* saying he'd beg…fuck, it had pushed Aled's buttons, whether he meant to do it or not.

Maybe this could be the breath of fresh air that Aled needed. Maybe he'd have a bit of fun, vent a little, and it would brush the cobwebs away enough to go after Melissa and try to work things out properly. Or it would wake up his latent sex drive enough that he had no option but to seek people like *angel23* out and get back into the field in some way. With or without Melissa.

Either way, it sounded like moving on, right?

Aled's phone buzzed and he opened the new message from *angel23* that simply said, *On my way.*

Waiting, he sent back. *Want anything?*

angel23: Dick would be nice.

gingerbiscuit: From the shop!

angel23: Do the staff have dick?

Aled glanced.

gingerbiscuit: No, all women.

angel23: Never mind. Latte if you're offering though, please :)

Aled got up and fetched the requested latte. It had started to rain outside, so cold and thick that it would be slush if the temperature dropped any further. He kept glancing back to see the street as he was served. There was no sign by the time he returned to the table, and no further messages, so he sat back and watched with an eagle eye. *angel23* probably looked nothing like his picture and yet Aled watched anyway. Maybe he'd be obvious — Aled had never met a trans man before — or maybe he'd be —

Aled's jaw sagged.

Just. Like. His. Picture.

A man walked out of the estate on the other side of the road. His hair was shockingly dark, so black it seemed to absorb the colour all around him. His skin, by contrast, was equally shockingly white, almost porcelain, and even at this distance, the dark spray of stubble across his jaw and neck was crystal clear. He wasn't tall, but he had long, confident strides. He wasn't wearing anything especially fashionable or eye-catching, but people were turning to look at him. At his face, Aled was sure. At his perfect, gorgeous, *beautiful* face.

He made a beeline for the coffee shop and Aled swallowed. *angel23* matched his picture perfectly. Flushed mouth, dark hair, dark eyes, as he pushed into the shop and his gaze flicked briefly around before landing on Aled.

He smiled.

Aled's chest caught at the slow, wide smile that bloomed and creased that paper-white skin. The creases put ten years on him, so he looked thirty instead of twenty, but when it faded, the years vanished again like a mirage. Aled gestured at the latte, feeling oddly numb as the stranger approached. He couldn't quite breathe.

Fuck, he was beautiful.

And fuck, did Aled want him.

"Aled?"

"Guilty."

A hand was stuck out. Long fingers. White as his face. Smooth, when Aled shook it, but for rough bumps on the palm where his knuckles lurked under the skin.

"Gabriel."

"Nice to meet you," Aled said and flicked his gaze down to the latte. "So — how fast can you drink that?"

Gabriel laughed. His voice was mid-range, but he had a high laugh. Almost musical. He sank down into the chair opposite and a foot ended up between Aled's under the table.

"Keen, aren't you?"

"Yeah, well, I was expecting at least a *bit* of exaggeration when it came to your photo," Aled mock-grumbled.

Gabriel took a sip of the coffee and licked his lips. Those near-black eyes raked Aled as if he was a specimen to be studied. But Aled could feel the familiar cool rush of adrenalin and confidence pooling in his system and met the stare head-on. Challenging. Demanding.

And Gabriel noticed, by the way he licked his bottom lip again.

"You're not what I imagined," he said slowly.

Aled quirked an eyebrow.

"You look like you have scheduled sex with your wife once a week, on Saturday nights, and it takes four minutes and thirty seconds."

He wanted to laugh. But something made him smirk instead and Gabriel shifted in his chair.

"Very specific," Aled drawled, testing the waters, and Gabriel fidgeted again.

"You, uh. You don't look like you want a three-course meal from a stranger on Grindr."

Reading from the script. A year out of the game and it was still the same thing that people noticed every time. They still set themselves up for the same surprise. Aled drained his cup, then leaned in to whisper.

"That's the thing about short ginger guys," he breathed. "We have a lot more to prove. And I am *very* good at proving it."

Gabriel's throat bobbed silently in his neck. Aled imagined it nudging the head of his dick, and grinned.

"You mentioned begging. I've never slept with anyone who hasn't been begging for more by the end of it."

Gabriel curled his fingers around Aled's arm and stroked the soft skin on the underside of his wrist. "Best find that alleyway, then."

"Mm, don't think so. Not in this rain. How far's your place?"

"Ten-minute walk."

"Five," Aled said, pushing back his chair. "Walk quickly."

In truth, he didn't really know what he wanted to do, or what he was doing. But there was adrenalin in his system. He could feel his body almost waking up, as though he was stepping out of the dark and into the light. Whatever else had happened this past year, he could smirk at an attractive man over a cup of coffee and have him breathless without lifting a finger. His eyes still had it. His voice could still rumble.

And Aled knew that was where his power lay. He wasn't conventionally attractive. The spare tyre was getting too big to just be a Saturday night burger. Ginger blokes weren't frequenting the covers of *Attitude* and *GQ* on a regular basis. Five seven was average height for a woman and he hadn't lifted anything heavier than a bag of shopping in more than ten years.

But he could drop his voice to the demanding purr of an arrogant master without a moment's thought. His mouth was a miracle worker and he could read a body better than a book. Even without Gabriel yanking on his sleeve to tow him out of the shop and threatening him with pain if he turned out to be vanilla after all, Aled could read the lust in that work of art of a body.

So he didn't wait for the flat.

It had stopped sleeting, but the sky was a furious black. They crossed the main road and were swallowed up by the estate again and, as they ducked between two blocks of flats, Aled caught an elbow and hauled Gabriel into the shadowed recess between two dumpsters, slamming him up against a thankfully locked fire door with enough force to crash the air right out of him, and seized his mouth in a hungry kiss.

"Fuck," Gabriel whispered when he could and Aled rubbed a thigh up between his legs. "Oh my God. *Fuck.*"

"What's the magic word?"

"*Please.*"

"Better," Aled chided, thumbing the button on Gabriel's jeans. There was a slip of skin brushing his knuckles. He could feel a rabbit-fast pulse against his wedding ring. "What do you want?"

"You to fuck me until it comes out my mouth."

Aled raised his eyebrows. "Yeah? Right here where your neighbours can see?"

"Don't care."

He popped the button and found nothing. No underwear. Just wiry hair and damp heat. Gabriel bucked against him as he explored, grinding down on Aled's thigh. Aled could feel—

"What you want me to call it?"

"What?"

He stroked the short length, thicker than usual but no sign of surgery. "This."

"S'my dick," Gabriel said breathlessly. "Thought you were good?"

Aled squeezed until Gabriel's voice cut off in a high whine.

"Don't get smart."

"You gonna shut me up?"

Aled bit him. Deep and hard, right in the juncture of his neck and shoulder. Hands clawed his shoulders and hips rose jerkily. It let him in, then he had two fingers buried to the knuckle in hot, wet fire.

"I know what to do with this. Question is, you want that first and the starter when we get home, or are you not a fan of appetisers on their own?"

Teeth caught Aled's ear. Sucked. Then broke away to whisper.

"I'm a traditionalist. Three courses means three. An appetiser would be four and that's just wrong."

Aled laughed. "Finger-fuck not enough for you?"

"I want your cock. Don't make me beg again."

"I'll make you beg whenever I want." Aled withdrew his fingers and yanked at the jeans. It was cold. The rain was barely holding off. The first cold drops pattered down as he pulled down his zip and pumped himself once, twice, to get from interested to in.

"You want this?"

"Fuck yes."

"Then ask nicely."

Gabriel swore but then arched his back. A leg hooked over Aled's hip. A hungry cunt touched at him and Aled held deliberately still. Kept his face blank. Cold. Controlled.

In charge.

"Please, God, fuck me, fuck me right here and right now —"

Aled pushed. Gabriel groaned. Deep. Guttural. Aled caught his mouth to shut him up and lost himself there. Two wet, welcoming spaces opening up to him as if they were built for his use. The scrape of brick on denim. The drag of hungry muscle when Gabriel didn't want to let him pull out. The warning tightness that stopped the head when he buried himself back inside, his dick just a little longer than Gabriel allowed for. The crash of thighs against his hips as he thrust. The whispers against his mouth —*faster, harder, more*—and the answering burst of energy in his spine.

It had been —

So long. Too long. The first fuck in a year and it was in an alleyway with a stranger. Rubbing a stranger's dick between his fingers. Hammering a stranger's cunt like it was familiar as home.

It had been too long.

He came in a lightning strike. Everything seized up. He buried teeth in a lip. Felt nails in his scalp. Squeezed until he felt the answering storm in Gabriel and the stuttered breathing and spasmodic tugging that said he was still good at sex.

Even if the act itself didn't take so long.

"There's your starter," he muttered hoarsely and pulled out. "Takes the edge off. Means you can savour the main course."

Gabriel's gaze was wide and dazed, but he smiled. Kissed him. It was messy and off-kilter. Hungry and wanting.

"There's cum in my jeans."

"Should have worn underwear then," Aled said, tucking himself away.

"Just gets in the way," Gabriel mumbled, then grinned. "So. I begged."

"You did."

"And I'll beg again if it'll get you into my flat and bending me over the bed."

Aled smirked, crowding Gabriel back into the wall for a hungry kiss. Gabriel's knees shivered and his hands fisted in Aled's jacket. The rain was lashing it down once more and Aled hadn't noticed.

"Tell you what," Aled whispered, lips brushing up Gabriel's jaw to his ear. "Your flat. Lose the clothes. And I'll clean you up with my tongue — *then* bend you over whatever surface you want and get you messy again. If you're good."

Gabriel pushed him. "And if I'm bad?"

Lust burst back into life like a button had been pressed. Aled seized. Gabriel hung in his grip, jaw slack, eyes staring.

"Don't be bad."

Gabriel licked his lips, leaned up and kissed him.

Chapter Four

"Fuck."

The chuckle against his ear—low, warm and almost smoky—sent shivers chasing the afterglow of the best orgasm Gabriel had had in days. He hummed, dragging his fingers across the floorboards as lips wrapped around his earlobe and sucked lightly.

"Fuck," he whispered again.

"We did, yes," came the deep reply, then tongue and teeth tugged at his earlobe before letting go and the weight spread out over his back moved.

Gabriel scowled and clenched. But it wasn't enough. Hips shifted. The messy slide of a soft cock slipping free was offset by the tug of a condom. Gabriel closed his eyes and grimaced at the sensation.

"Okay?"

"No. You should have stayed inside."

If the chuckle had been dirty, seedy and completely fuckable all on its own, the lighter laugh was oddly warm. Gabriel twisted his head to peer out from under heavy eyelids and admired the view of Aled propped up on his forearms, nose tracking Gabriel's sweaty shoulder in tantalising strokes, freckly biceps bulging under a round layer of fat.

"Next time," Gabriel murmured sleepily, "you can forget the rubber."

"You wish."

"You did the first time."

"Yeah, and that was a cock-up."

"Mm. Can I get some more cock up..."

It had been swift, brutal and exactly what he'd needed. The minute Gabriel had closed the front door, Aled had slammed him up against it and ripped his jeans off. Then when Gabriel had tried to kiss him and persuade him to head for bed and a blowjob, Aled had just swept out his feet from under him and they'd both gone tumbling to the floor.

And *fuck,* it had been a good one.

Aled was heavy. Hairy. He was short and stocky, like a soft barrel, and he'd held Gabriel under him effortlessly, his chest sticking to Gabriel's back as they'd moved. Gabriel had been loosened up by the shag in the alley, but the cum Aled had left behind — apparently by mistake — had been half-dried and caught. It had been the perfect blend of smooth and not, and as Aled pressed a bristly kiss to the back of Gabriel's neck, Gabriel could have purred.

"Where can I bin this?"

"What?"

"The rubber."

"Floor."

"Bin, you layabout."

"My flat, my rules," Gabriel grumbled, then pushed. Aled sat back on his heels to let him go and Gabriel followed, plucking the used condom from his fingers only to drop it on the floor. Aled's thigh was hot and sticky between Gabriel's legs and his mouth tasted like coffee. Gabriel sucked on his lower lip, sliding higher on his lap until that soft, used cock was resting against him. Heavy. Hot.

Promisingly thick.

"Dessert?" he whispered against Aled's mouth, their lips catching with every syllable.

"You'll be so lucky…"

"Or that good."

"Only did the V."

"But you did it twice, so it counts," Gabriel chided and bit the lower lip. He sucked. *Hard.* And the cock caught between them thickened just a little more.

This time, the quiet "fuck" wasn't Gabriel's.

"Come to bed," Gabriel whispered. "Starter in the alley and main course on the floor — let's at least be classy about dessert."

Aled laughed, nudging his jaw against Gabriel's. He needed a shave and Gabriel ground his cheek against the sandpapery texture, sparks of electricity crackling across his face from the contact.

"Oh, you like that?"

Gabriel hummed agreeably and reeled in a shaky breath when Aled rubbed those sparks against his neck. Gabriel could come on a love bite alone. This —

"You're getting wet again. Well. Wetter."

"Gonna do something about it?"

The chuckle was back. Dark and dirty. A hand gripped the back of his neck and Gabriel breathed out in a long, high whimper as roughness scraped down to his shoulder and a bruise was sucked into being.

"I'm not one for something sucking on me when I'm soft," Aled murmured. "So how about you open those knees for me a third time and I put this to work on *your* cock instead?"

Gabriel bit his lip until it ached. God, have that — that — *grit*, scouring at him like it would rip his skin off as well as get him off? Fuck, he wanted to ride it. Wanted to just lock his thighs around Aled's head and hold him there until he'd rubbed Gabriel's dick right off with that broken glass of a would-be beard.

A hand patted his backside and a single finger pushed underneath to toy with his well-fucked cunt. Gabriel wriggled. It flexed and the cool back of a fingernail rubbed gently against him, almost like a kiss.

"Take it that's a yes?" Aled asked.

"Bed."

Aled still needed towing by the hand. He was entirely naked, light freckles dusting every inch of skin, including his prick. He had once been stocky and muscular, now hidden under a spare tyre and thick thighs. The jaw could have cut diamond even without the sinful stubble, and his smirk turned Gabriel's legs to water as he was crowded down onto the mattress in a tangle of limbs. Aled's cock was semi-hard, thick but not yet rising from its crop of curls, and it nestled comfortably against Gabriel's hip. He glanced down and grinned. Curtains matched the carpets.

"You're too high."

"Open up, then."

He didn't bother trying to be sexy about it. Just dragged himself up to the pillows and opened his legs, rubbing one hand down the crease of hip and thigh and adjusting his already well-satisfied — and well up for another go — dick. If there was one thing Gabriel liked about his physical origins, it was this. Aled might need some recovery time. Gabriel? He was all sorted.

And if Aled didn't hurry the fuck up, after all that face-rubbing, Gabriel would be gagging for it, too.

"Ah-ah," Aled chided, catching his wrist. "That's mine."

"What's — oh, *fuck*!"

He'd expected Aled to do what most guys willing to blow Gabriel tried to do. And sure, he didn't object to being eaten out. It was nice enough and it was a great warm-up for the good stuff.

But Aled didn't go there.

He went straight for Gabriel's cock.

"Fuck-fuck-fuck — "

It was like having an entire bottle of heated lube poured over his dick and nowhere else. And when Aled sucked, Gabriel lost his voice entirely. He whined, fisting both hands in the sheets as Aled explored his labia with the very tip of his tongue, then cocooned his dick in that hot, wet heat once more. And again, and again, and again —

He was already on fire before the stubble ever came into play. And when it did, it was like his entire leg was consumed in the flames. He nearly kicked Aled in the side of the head, then was tortured through a second pass with two hard, heavy hands pinning his hips down to the bed. Soon, all Gabriel could hear was himself. Swearing. Gasping. Begging. As the fire was scraped across his inner thighs, every muscle below his chest jumping in desperation, the water soothing it only to have all the sensation dragged back into his straining cock. After the first, Gabriel thought he was going to dissolve — but then Aled did it again, and again, and again —

He barely noticed coming the first time. He only felt the sharp bite delivered to his stomach minutes later.

And by the time he realised that the pressure on his cock was Aled's body and not his tongue, and that he'd missed his chance of sucking off the shaft that was fucking him through the mattress, it was almost over.

Gabriel didn't care.

He just hooked an arm around Aled's neck, drew him down and bit his ear in furious retribution.

Because somewhere in there, that smug son of a bitch had managed to glove up again.

Chapter Five

When Aled woke up, he was alone.

He knew it immediately, though he couldn't put his finger on why. But as he stretched and explored enough to find Gabriel's bathroom and have a piss, he realised it was the total and complete silence permeating the flat. It was unnaturally quiet.

Admittedly, Aled hadn't done much looking around when they'd stumbled in off the street and fucked in the middle of the floor, but he'd seen enough to know it wasn't a big flat. Even Gabriel sitting and quietly reading a book should have given away his presence *somehow*.

A cursory search after aforementioned piss confirmed it—Gabriel was gone.

Aled stretched again, ironing the kinks out of his back. It hadn't been anything monumental, really. They had staggered in wrapped around each other and he'd fucked Gabriel into the bare wooden floor right behind the door. Then he'd sucked Gabriel off and fucked him through his orgasm. Aled must have fallen asleep after that.

They were just clumsy, messy shags.

But he felt...good. Tired, but a good tired, for the first time in months. His skin was buzzing gently, like the satisfied hum after a hard workout and a hot bath. The ache wasn't in his chest, for once. He didn't feel like he needed to sleep even more. He felt—happy. Positive. *Bright.*

God, maybe Tom was right. Maybe a bit of Gabriel *was* good for the soul.

He padded back to the bedroom to find his briefs, and also found a note on the bedside table. Gabriel's handwriting was scratchy and hurried—*gone 2 werk feel free 2 rade fridge*—and Aled wondered what he actually did for a living. The flat was obviously rented, the décor too bland and neutral for any actual, living human being to willingly put in their own home, but then there was no roommate evident, so Aled guessed he wasn't still a student or pulling part-time shifts at some bar somewhere.

Fuelled by curiosity and time, Aled went exploring properly. He was suddenly intensely curious about this trans guy with all the confidence and swagger of any cis bloke Aled had ever met before. He'd always imagined trans men would be a bit shy in bed. Hesitant. Less up for one-night stands.

Not on Grindr with a waiting list of potential shags.

The flat was only three rooms—a small main room, with a kitchenette jammed in next to a crowded living space, a bedroom with a stunning view of the brick alley between the two blocks of flats and a bathroom with a serious case of black mould sprouting from one corner of the ceiling. The house-proud part of Aled shivered at the desperate need to repair and repaint almost every aspect of the place.

Gabriel's bedroom told him very little, but his bathroom was a weird mash-up of products that reminded Aled of his own before his wife had walked out. The deodorants and razors were men's, but there was a box of tampons on the side and a set of bath bombs that were distinctly at aimed at women, judging by the flowers all over the packaging. If not for the single bedroom and lack of anyone else's clothes, Aled could have been convinced of a girlfriend, or at least a female roommate. And when he found a half-empty tub of *Slimming World* diet shake powder in the bathroom cabinet, he wondered if that was just a thing that trans people did. Keep the best bits of the wrong gender and adopt all the other bits of the right one? He'd have to ask.

He borrowed some of the lemon and lime shower gel for a quick scrub-down, and was pleasantly surprised by the luxuriously fluffy towels, before dressing again and wandering into the main room. The kitchenette looked like it was supposed to house a bodybuilder, with all the high-protein foods and shakes everywhere, and Aled suspected that Gabriel was probably the only person in the building who owned a copy of *Men's Health* to actually read the articles instead of just gawk at the pictures. There was no booze in the place, but a stash of cigarettes that could put a newsagent's to shame was hidden in a cupboard between a tower of baked beans and a thousand packets of instant soup.

The living room area was the most revealing, by the corkboard covered in photographs of the countryside, the filthy mountain bike propped up in the corner and the bundle of cycling maps from the Ordnance Survey folks on the coffee table. Aled groaned. Gabriel was one of those outdoors types. And a *cyclist*. Christ, Aled gave himself bonus points for not deliberately running them over when he encountered cyclists. At least it was a mountain bike, not a road bike, and — he leafed through the maps and pulled out a couple of orange tickets, months old — it looked like Gabriel was more in the habit of taking the bike on the train somewhere nice than cycling up the A650 and carving up the traffic.

Nice-ish, anyway. Why would he have taken the bike to Sheffield, of all places?

Aled put the pile back the way he found it. He ought to go. Gabriel had made no mention of coming back, and it was nearly six in the evening. Aled still had to get the bus back to Wakefield. He picked up his jacket from where Gabriel had shoved it off his shoulders halfway to the bedroom. He patted it down for his keys and phone, then hesitated.

Phone.

Should he…?

The *intention* had just been a quick shag with someone who was a bit interesting and had a gorgeous mouth. But Aled felt good. Unreasonably good, for a quick shag. Gabriel had been responsive in all the right places and the little whimper he'd made when Aled had thrust into him for the first time had been sensational.

And, of course, there was the way he'd responded to being held against the wall.

Aled swallowed. To hell with it. If he left his number and Gabriel never called, so what? And if he did, then maybe they could do it again sometime. Either way, Aled wasn't going to lose by leaving it, was he?

He found a permanent marker in one of the kitchen drawers and paced back into the bedroom to add his number to the poorly spelled note Gabriel had left him.

Then Aled corrected his spelling, and left.

* * * *

Aled lived on the Darnley estate, about fifteen minutes down from the bus station. It wasn't an especially long way, so, in light of the bitterly cold but gloriously bright and dry weather, he hunched deeper into his coat and decided to walk it and break it up with a cup of coffee in town on the way.

And with that in mind, rang Tom.

"Aled? The fuck, mate, what's up? Something wrong?"

Aled didn't usually directly speak to Tom on the phone. Although they got along perfectly well, and Aled certainly considered Tom a good friend, he was and always would be Suze's boyfriend before he was Aled's friend. Unless it was *about* Suze, Tom and Aled rarely spoke or met up without her.

So his instant jump from surprise to concern wasn't too big a leap.

Still —

"Hi, Tom, how are you? Fine, thanks, nice weather," Aled deadpanned.

"Shove off."

Predictable.

"Just wanted to let you know, I owe your brother a pub of pints."

"Yeah?" Tom laughed. "You meet up with his angel?"

"Yep. Gabriel."

"You're kidding."

"Nope."

"The Archangel Gabriel, fuck me."

"Well, I fucked him, actually, but semantics…"

Tom laughed again and Aled heard him sitting back in whatever chair he was in. "Do you some good, did he?"

"Yeah," Aled confessed. "I'll only say this once, but you were right."

Tom whooped.

"I needed that. I feel good, for once."

"And you've realised that it's for once?"

"Eh?"

"Come off it, mate, you've been feeling nothing or crap since your missus walked. You feel good now. That throwing the last year into a bit of perspective for you?"

Aled grimaced, suddenly remembering the *other* reason he and Tom didn't speak alone often. Tom made Suze look cuddly and empathetic with personal advice.

But—

"I can't deny that," he admitted quietly. "It wasn't even the shag, you know? It was just…feeling close to someone again. Like that."

"Bit too mushy for me, mate."

"Oh, fuck off, Tom, you act like a kicked puppy whenever Suze gets sent to the New York office."

"I do not."

"I'll film it next time," Aled said mildly. "Point is, I feel good. Really good." He was leaving the town centre and crossed the road to detour for coffee before heading home. "It's woken everything up a bit, I reckon."

"Good. You gonna fuck him again?"

Aled rolled his eyes. "I don't know."

"You left your number."

"I said, I don't know."

"Which means you totally left your number, because you are a romantic, and you decided to bang a guy based on his *eye* colour."

"It was his mouth!"

"You waxed lyrical about his eyes for five minutes, Aled. Face it. You. Are. A. Girl."

"I'm a girl who had a phenomenal shag this morning with someone straight out of a beauty magazine, so that would make me the success of the day and you the sad loser sitting around in his bunny slippers."

The distinct rub of carpet on fuzz met his ears before Tom grouchily said, "Barefoot."

"Yeah, now you've slipped them off."

"You know what, fuck this. I preferred you mopey and depressed."

"Yeah, whatever, mate," Aled said as he pushed open the coffee shop door. "Just thank your brother for me. He's more useful than you."

He hung up to Tom's indignant assessment of him as an ungrateful bastard and beamed at the barista. It was absurd but...he *did* feel as good as he'd said. He felt awake, like he'd been drowsy and tired for a very long time, and now he'd had a good sleep and a shot of energy all at once. And Aled wasn't thick — sex did that to the brain, chemically speaking — but he'd take what he could get from it. And, grudgingly, he had to admit that Tom and Suze were right. He'd been depressed. There was no denying it...and no shame in it, Aled felt. Of course he'd been depressed. His wife had left him.

But now...maybe this was the way to actually get control of his life back. Clear out his system — maybe see Gabriel again, maybe see some other men and women—and once he was feeling better, feeling happier, feeling more confident, he could get a grip on everything again. Be that go after her and finally work on their problems, instead of burying his head in the sand, or be that…

Not.

But feeling better, Aled thought maybe he *could* work it out with Melissa now. The day she'd left, he'd simply stood and watched her go, and physically felt his heart breaking in his chest. They'd never really rowed. There wasn't a screaming argument, complete with slamming doors and breaking plates. There wasn't some climax of a story, no coming to a head.

She'd said, *'You'll regret it if you don't. You'll be old and alone, and you'll regret it.'*

He'd said, *'No, I won't.'*

And she'd quietly got up and left.

And never come back.

Aled had never confronted her about it. They'd never had that final argument. They'd split up in this strange limbo, where they had never finished the disagreement that had broken them down.

And Aled knew *why* she'd gone. It wasn't that he didn't understand *why*. It was just that he'd hoped that it wouldn't keep her away. As the months had slipped by, he'd kept hoping that maybe today, maybe this week, maybe next, she would come back and they could finish what they'd started.

Only she never had.

Now, with that energetic buzz thrumming through his veins, Aled thought that maybe this was the kick-start he needed. He could ring her up and they could have lunch and talk about it. Maybe the year apart had been necessary, to brush the cobwebs off their marriage and re-evaluate. Sometimes, putting a project on hold and coming back to it later could bring ways around the problem into view that couldn't be seen before. Maybe she wouldn't be so adamant that they had to do things the traditional way. Maybe he'd have learned from the quiet and the loneliness and be more open to what she needed.

Maybe they finally had a chance to —

Aled turned into the street and stopped dead.

His house was barely visible from the corner, sitting as it was on the junction between Henry Street and Plumpton Road. But the car parked outside it — the very familiar little car that used to sit in his driveway and used to contain a spare jacket in the boot for him and had a scuff mark on the door from where he'd once drunkenly opened it too wide and hit the garage wall — was perfectly visible.

As was the woman leaning against the boot, head down, texting.

Melissa.

Chapter Six

When he was fourteen, one of the girls at school had called Gabriel a professional prostitute.

At the time, Gabriel had been hurt. Now, after eight hours on his feet being polite to arseholes, he wondered if he hadn't made a crap career choice by not putting his phone number on toilet walls. At least he'd get more money to suck suits off than help them figure out how to use the self-checkout machines. And they'd probably be nicer about it.

He hated the itchy uniform. He hated the customers. He hated the seventeen-year-old team leader who gave him speeches about the importance of correctly stacked shelves. And the one good thing about his job — the weekdays security guard who liked to stick his dick in anything that wasn't his wife — had been sacked last week for being caught with his trousers down in the stockroom.

Even Aled fucking him into a coma couldn't keep Gabriel in a good mood for eight hours of stacking shelves and smiling at Susan while she screamed that he needed to honour her out-of-date vouchers.

It was dark when he left and he headed for the bus stop. During the day he'd walk back, but Gabriel could pass all he wanted—he was still a five-foot-five white guy with a girly walk. Even after he'd managed to scrub 'girl' off his face, 'gay' was still well and truly tattooed there.

Which meant when his phone started ringing—an iPhone, a Christmas gift from Kevin—he was reluctant to take it out of his pocket. He slid it free with the intention of just silencing it but then grinned when he saw the name, so plugged his earphones in and swiped the call open.

"Hey, Kevin."

"Well, hello there. Nice of you to stay in touch."

Gabriel sighed dramatically, but it didn't wipe the grin off his face. He reached the bus stop and settled into the seat in the shelter, hunching his shoulders against the cold and any prying eyes.

"Nice holiday?"

"Except for the radio silence. You good?"

Gabriel had known Kevin for three years. Kevin knew *everything*. Sometimes the question meant myriad things—who'd he fucked, what he'd taken, if he'd been to the clinic lately, what did he need, where was he, who was he with—and other times, it just meant...

"I'm good."

"You working?"

Gabriel raised his eyebrows. "What, right now? Just left. Waiting for the bus."

Kevin snorted. "Fuck the bus. I'll give you a ride."

"I bet you will—"

"Can it, you tart. You on the main road?"

"Yeah."

"Stay there. Give me five minutes."

"If you don't beat the bus, I'll get on it."

He was sworn at, called a cheeky bitch for his language, then the call cut out. Gabriel smirked. He usually didn't like terms like that, but it never seemed to matter what Kevin said. He slid the phone away again and settled back against the glass to wait.

It was Saturday night and the main road was busy. Other buses trundled past. Most folks were heading the other way, into the city proper. A cluster of blokes were staggering out of a taxi and weaving their way towards the strip club. A cluster of birds on the other side of the road were loudly jeering at them. One lass had already got her tits out and it was only half past nine.

Ah, Leeds.

Gabriel wasn't from Leeds, but it was like everywhere else he'd ever lived, really. Just people being messy and dirty and fun and shit all at once. He didn't like his neighbours much and he didn't like being so obviously gay, but everywhere else had been much the same. One day, he didn't doubt he'd move on again. But for the moment, it was nice. He had his own place. He had Kevin and Judith for family and several regulars for fun. And the queer scene was much bigger than he'd first assumed. He'd had his first sauna sex in Leeds, so it would always hold a special place in his heart.

But the best part was Kevin.

The Citroen that purred up in front of the bus stop was a family car. Empty baby seat in the back. Bike rack on the roof. Muddy. Dented. The grimy outline of a butterfly sticker or five having been scraped off the paintwork. But the bodybuilder who peered out of the window at him with those sharp, appraising eyes was like a scene from a porn film and Gabriel deliberately bent down to the passenger window like the so-called victim about to be kidnapped.

"Hi," he said. "Looking for someone?"

"Christ, you're a slag," Kevin said and chuckled. "Get in. If you want some dick that badly, you can stay over and I'll fuck you in the morning."

Gabriel grinned.

Kevin was a sadist. They fucked sometimes — and most often when Gabriel was feeling low or dangerously out of control, and needed an endorphin shot and a heavy punishment to wrench his brain back online. But more often, they were simply...

Friends seemed too loose. Family seemed a little awkward given Kevin had once kept him chained in the basement for a whole week, earning food with sex. But Gabriel trusted Kevin like nobody else, and if he'd come to Leeds to get away, he'd stayed for Kevin. For walking round to Kevin's after work if there'd been creepers around and letting himself in to sleep in the basement until morning. For company at shitty action films that Judith refused to see. For boxes of leftover chilli.

And yes, for sex so intense it literally hurt, but Kevin was one of Gabriel's few regulars for whom it wasn't just sex.

So he grinned when Kevin called him a slag, and slid into the passenger seat anyway.

"You want your home or mine?"

"Mine," Gabriel said. "I got laid this morning so I'm good. You?"

"Probably made another bloody baby."

"Hey, the lady gets what she wants..."

"The lady doesn't need more babies!"

Gabriel laughed and made fun of Kevin the family man. He'd been married when they'd met, but both Lily and Grace were under three. And the sex had been a lot more savage on Kevin's part when his sub had been heavily pregnant or nursing a newborn. Gabriel kind of liked it—but then he kind of liked being able to walk the next day, too.

"Well, if you want a risk-free cunt, you know where to find me."

"Risk-free, my arse…"

"That too."

Kevin's teeth flashed as he laughed. He'd shaved his head and Gabriel loudly mourned the dreadlocks. It earned him an obscene grope and a threat of a belt, and he shrugged it off and asked who the slag was, after all.

"So who was the fuck? Michael?"

"Nope. He's still in the doghouse after that girl comment."

Kevin whistled. "Fair play. So who was the lucky guy? New one, old one?"

"New."

"Good?"

"Very. Knew how to blow me proper."

"Nillice," Kevin said approvingly.

"Just a Grindr hookup."

"Regular?"

"Dunno. He seemed like he was just after the one day, but then he fucked me three times and fell asleep in my bed, so—" Gabriel waved a hand. "Whatever. I'm going to message him again."

He let Kevin pull in at a drive-through for KFC, then drop him off at the flats. Kevin was a wall of a man and it helped flashing him around the place occasionally. The flats weren't exactly refined. He waved to Them

Downstairs as he let himself in the communal door and studiously pretended not to see the blazing row between Y'Bastard and Fat Slag in the stairwell. One of the teenagers on the second floor called him a faggot. He flipped them off and rummaged for his keys as he kept heading up.

Welfare had its downsides.

Still, the door was heavy and had a good lock. Once it was bolted and the chain pulled across, Gabriel shrugged out of his hoodie with a sigh, texted Kevin a thanks and rolled his head on his neck until things creaked. He stretched. He could have done with Aled's marathon fuck in the evening rather than during the day, but he wasn't going to turn down a free screw, no matter what time it was.

Speaking of which—

He'd left Aled asleep in bed to go to work, but even a cursory glance around the living room said he'd left. His clothes weren't scattered all over the floor, for one. Gabriel's were. And the abandoned condom. He grinned and threw it away before heading for the bathroom. The shower cubicle was still damp, but the used towel dry. He was long gone.

Oh well. Message it is.

He showered first and wanked away the last traces of the fuck. They'd have to negotiate the whole condom thing if Aled turned into a regular, but whatever. There were a couple of brands he didn't mind so much. Long as Aled wasn't totally into cheap off-the-supermarket-shelf crap, they'd work something out.

He wandered around drip-drying for a while and cleaning up. Getting the cum stain off the floor, putting his clothes in for a wash, even redoing the bed. He didn't have to work again until the middle of next week, which meant plenty of time for better activities. Which meant being prepared.

And if he hadn't been preparing for a good time, he'd never have found it.

But as he stooped to scoop up stray socks from the bedroom floor, the slip of black by the bedpost caught his eye. Black leather or black boxers by the bed were normal, but this was a rough, corduroy-type fabric and Gabriel frowned at the wallet like it might offer an explanation for its presence.

"What the—"

It was heavy. A bundle of crumpled notes peered up at him when he flipped it open and the bank cards were made out to Mr A. Z. Evans.

Then he found the driving license—and an old, terrible photo of a scrawny ginger teenager in far-too-large glasses—and cracked up laughing.

Oh, Aled would owe him the mother of all fucks if he didn't put *this* baby on Grindr.

Still—

"Hello, new regular," Gabriel muttered to himself and went to find his phone. "Let's bring the cock back to the henhouse, shall we?"

Chapter Seven

Just like that, the confidence was gone.

It evaporated out of his system like water in a desert. The buzzing stopped. The pleasant hum dried up. Everything shrivelled at the very sight of her – her hair, her shoes, her fingers on the phone, *everything* – and Aled suddenly wanted nothing more than to run away.

But then she looked up. And across a whole street, their eyes locked. Just like always. His heart twisted. Just like always.

And just like always, he was rendered helpless.

So, heart sinking into his stomach, Aled kept walking.

"Melissa." He tried for a smile. "What brings you here?"

Melissa's smile seemed equally forced.

He hadn't actually seen his wife since the day she'd walked out, now fractionally over a year ago. There'd been phone calls – him trying to persuade her to come back, her trying to persuade him to let go – and a flurry of emails about purely pragmatic matters, but he'd not *seen* her in a year.

And she'd changed.

Melissa, the whole time Aled had known her, had always been...well, the kind of girl he liked. "The girl on fire." That was what Suze had called her. She was a tall woman with long reddish-blonde hair and Aled had first seen her winning the fifteen-hundred-metre race for the school, way back when they were fourteen years old. He'd wanted to know her name then and there and he'd wanted to marry her and be with her forever before he'd reached his fifteenth birthday.

The girl on fire was a good way to describe her. The girl good at everything, who could have done anything. She'd gotten top marks in every exam she'd ever sat, she had a degree in neuroscience and was up to her neck in research for a PhD seeking to determine whether gender identity disorders could be identified in the brain prior to their conscious realisation...and all before Aled had even finally given up hope of being a student forever and had gotten his first job as a marketing intern. She could hold the knowledge of the known universe in her head, while Aled was tearing his hair out trying to make Microsoft Excel add up properly. She could see the fine detail and the bigger picture all at once, and Aled couldn't figure out how to format a CV nicely.

In short, Melissa was brilliant, beautiful and...not the same woman that he'd married.

Aled supposed that there was his error.

All Aled had wanted was that brilliant, beautiful woman to be *his* brilliant, beautiful woman. He wanted to be able to feel like a manly superhero every now and then for rescuing her from spiders in the bath. He wanted to be able to beam stupidly next to her in her degree photograph and smugly say that his wife wasn't fussing about what colour scheme to use in the bathroom but was trying to stop transgender kids from being tortured by their own bodies going through puberty. He wanted to watch her rant and rave about idiotic opinions in her field that were miles of out his league, then make her feel better by calling Professor Whatshisface an ignorant old twat and offer her the latest crime drama, freshly recorded from the night before. He wanted her to smile at him like he was her lovable oaf of a boyfriend and see in him the warm, fun, light-hearted side of life that never made it into stuffy university halls and clinically cold labs.

He hadn't wanted her to get older.

Because eventually, of course, she had. They both had. And while Aled's position on family had never changed, Melissa's — slowly but surely — had.

The girl on fire would never have dreamed about getting married and having kids before she was forty, because there was a world to be saved, a career to be had and if her hapless boyfriend wanted a baby, they could adopt one. And he could change the nappies.

But little by little, she had changed. Slowly, she had wanted to be married and have Aled's last name. Gradually, she had started talking about children. Suddenly, she wasn't taking the pill anymore and she kept frowning worriedly at pregnancy test kits and talking about ticking clocks even though she was only twenty-nine, thirty, thirty-one. And Aled had —

He was ashamed to admit it now. Knew that really it would have only made things worse had they actually had a baby. Because he would have hated being a father and having that responsibility, and she would have hated him for not wanting anything to do with their child, and things would have fallen apart, only with a life in the middle torn in two between its unprepared parents.

But Aled had loved his wife more than a hypothetical baby and hadn't thought it through. Hadn't sat down and really *realised* that having a baby just because his wife wanted one was unfair on all of them. Hadn't thought of the consequences if he *did* get her pregnant—or if he didn't. So he'd said yes. He'd gone along with it. Gone with her to the doctor and the hospital and the fertility clinic, gone through test after test after test and watched her relief when they said she was perfectly fertile.

And watched her dissolve when his results had come back with quite the opposite result.

Aled was never going to have children.

That was the cold, hard truth of it. His sperm weren't fit for purpose. Even with drugs, even with IVF, they simply weren't capable of successful fertilisation. He wasn't ever going to be a father. There was nothing that they could do.

Melissa had cried. The doctor had been sympathetic, referring him to a counselling service and a fostering charity and suggesting even perhaps an in-family surrogacy, if Aled had siblings willing to help them. Saying it wasn't anything to be ashamed of, that lots of men had problems with fertility, that it didn't make him any less of a man, that he was otherwise perfectly healthy, that fatherhood wasn't about DNA.

Aled had felt nothing.

It sounded awful, but he hadn't cared. He hadn't wanted children in the first place and being told it was never going to happen meant *nothing* to him. They might as well have said he'd never grow a third arm. He didn't care. He had honestly told Melissa that he was fine with the result and if she really wanted a baby, maybe they could foster. Or get a cat.

She'd walked out less than a month later.

And now here she was, back on the front path like she'd only been away at one of her conferences. Only she'd cut her hair into a little bob that she'd never had before. Her features were gently accentuated with makeup, when she'd never bothered in all the years he'd known her. And she was wearing earrings he'd never seen before. Diamond ones. Shaped like little hearts, straight out of an expensive jewellers' window.

"You've found someone else," Aled croaked.

Melissa blinked and pursed her lips. "So much for small talk," she said weakly.

"So you have?"

"How have you been?" she asked. "Lovely weather we're having. Does Mrs Finch next door still have that disgusting old cat? And yes. By the way. I have."

Aled leaned back against the car, feeling sick. She'd found someone else. Of *course* she had. She was the girl on fire. Everyone would want to be Melissa's new husband—even some women would want that. What had Aled expected?

Well, this. But he hadn't *wanted* it.

"Why are you here," he said blankly. It was barely even a question.

Melissa's mouth pinched downwards. "I—well, here." She held out a brown envelope, unmarked and thick with papers when Aled took it from her. "The thing is, we're…well, we're still married, Aled. And Jack and I—"

"Jack."

"Yes."

"As in, Jack, the consultant neurologist who worked on your PhD project with you."

Melissa pinked. "Yes, you remember Jack. Well, the thing this, we…we want to start a family. And Jack's a bit traditional and wants to be married before we have any children—"

"So did you," Aled said in a hollow voice.

"We were young," Melissa said quietly. "We didn't think it through, Aled, neither of us did. And we both changed. If I'd thought for a minute that I'd have wanted children, I certainly wouldn't have married *you*."

The joke fell flat and Aled said nothing. He started down at the envelope, understanding but not wanting to.

"Divorce papers," he said finally.

Melissa sighed. "Yes."

"You want a divorce."

"We've been separated for a year."

"It's just a year! How can you want to marry someone else in just a—"

"I've known Jack a long—"

"Did you cheat on me?" Aled demanded. "Were you—"

"No!" she snapped. "You know I didn't! You knew about everyone else and Jack wasn't one of them! But I know him and I know what I want and I want at least the option to get married again!"

"So that's it? You're just giving up on us?"

"I haven't even seen you in that year. What 'us' is left?"

"That's not my fault!" Aled shouted. "You walked out with two suitcases and I never saw you again! You never wanted to try again!"

"Try what?" she asked. "Aled, I—I want to hold my own babies in my arms. I wanted them to be *your* babies. And when they said it would never happen and *you* said you'd rather just get a cat than a baby... I'm sorry. I really am. I never meant to hurt you and if I had known when we were kids that *I'd* want kids, then I would never have let it go so far."

Aled wanted to not believe her. He wanted her to be some sadistic bitch who'd fucked him over on purpose, because then he could have just hated her, loathed her, thrown her papers back in her face and told her to go fuck herself, fuck Jack and fuck her divorce lawyer in some sick, wealthy threesome for good measure. He could have been angry. He could hate. And he would have known what to do with hating her.

But she was *Melissa*. As brilliant and beautiful as the very first time he'd seen her, and all he wanted to do was kiss her and beg her to come home. He hadn't wanted her to go. And he still didn't want her to walk away — even though she'd long since left him behind. He clutched the envelope so hard that it crumpled, and found his vision blurring.

"Melissa, please —"

"Oh, Aled. I'm so sorry. But you know we can't fix this. I want to — to hold my little boy or my little girl in my arms. I want to have family holidays in trashy places like the Algarve because it's too much bother to take a five-year-old to Venice. I want to shout at my teenagers and say they all look like me and it's better than them looking like their father. I *need* that, Aled. And you — you don't want any of it."

"I just wanted *you*," Aled croaked and hated the crack in his voice. "Fuck's sake, Melissa, we were fine. We were perfect! And now — now —"

"We've changed," Melissa whispered. "Or at least I have. And I'm so sorry, Aled, but...I need to move on.

I do still love you, but it's not enough. I won't contest anything. I won't try to take your money or your house. I'll just walk away. But I need that divorce certificate to do it."

Aled swallowed and looked down at the envelope in his shaking hand. "Just go."

"Aled —"

"Just *go*, Lissa. Please, just — just go."

There was a pause, then her shoes slowly receded down the path and he heard the beep of the central locking. It was still familiar, a year after he'd last heard it, the morning after his thirty-second birthday. Thirty minutes after she'd asked if he would ever want a baby and he'd asked if they couldn't just get a baby cat instead.

"Aled, I — I know I hurt you and I'm so sorry. I hope…I hope you find someone else. I really do. And I hope when you do, maybe…maybe we can talk sometimes? Try and be friends, at least?"

Aled shook his head and didn't move until he heard her car door slam and the tyres crunch as they pulled away from the house.

Then he cried.

He let himself in and sank down onto the stairs, sobbing like a child. He'd lost her. He'd truly lost her, for good. She wanted a divorce. She was marrying someone else. Because he couldn't give her children, because he didn't want a baby, because he wasn't what she needed anymore. He'd failed. He'd married the girl he'd loved since he was fourteen years old, and he'd failed to even begin to be what she'd needed. And now she was going off into the sunset with another man and another man's hypothetical baby, and he was supposed to be comforted that she wasn't going to demand her half of the house, her half of his money, her half of everything?

Almost on cue, his mobile started ringing. It would be Suze and her sixth sense, he was sure, but when he fumbled it out of his pocket, an unfamiliar number was calling. Scrubbing his sleeve over his face, he took a deep breath and croaked, "Aled," into the opened call. *Please let it be work.* Please let it be something to take his mind off everything that had gone so badly, badly wrong.

It wasn't work.

"If your last name is Evans," said a voice, "then you left your wallet here."

Aled blinked. "Gabriel?"

"Guilty. So, are you? Aled Evans?"

"I—you have my wallet?" Aled croaked, patting down his pockets. *Shit!*

"Yup, was under the bed. Bank cards, driving license with a photo that actually does your hair justice and a Caffè Nero loyalty card. You're only a stamp away. Want to buy me coffee sometime?"

Aled cracked a watery smile. "Are you asking me out?"

"I'm asking for free coffee, don't get ideas. So do you want me to drop it off, or—"

"Um, no, no, I'll come and get it." Aled sniffed and checked his face in the hall mirror. "Can I pop over now?"

"Sure. You okay? You sound congested."

"Hay fever."

"In January?" Gabriel asked sceptically. "Are you a florist?"

"What?" It surprised a laugh out of Aled. "Um, no, I—" Shit, why *would* he have hay fever?

"Ah, knocking off a florist, gotcha. Come and get your Caffè Nero card. I even have antihistamines somewhere in the bathroom cabinet, so you might get double lucky."

Aled thanked him and hung up before saving the number under *Gabriel Grindr* and going to wash his face. Gabriel would be sunny enough for both of them. Maybe Aled could talk his way into staying the night. Maybe it would make him feel better and forget about how badly he'd failed.

On the way out of the door, he picked up the brown envelope and threw it into the recycling bin.

Chapter Eight

Gabriel opened the door, wallet in hand — and paused.

Hay fever, his fragrant behind. Aled had been crying. His eyes were bloodshot and his voice had been hoarse on the phone. Something had happened since he'd fucked Gabriel through the mattress that morning and Gabriel felt a twinge of guilt.

He'd fucked his fair share of cheating husbands and closeted queers. There were a lot of guys who figured men like Gabriel didn't really count as *men,* so were safe for some queer experimentation. He hadn't taken Aled to be one of them — too aggressively confident, too utterly comfortable — but perhaps he'd called it wrong. Perhaps this was a much bigger deal for Aled than it was for Gabriel.

Still, Gabriel knew better than to open an emotional can of worms with a strange man in his flat, so he opted for humour.

"I might have taken a picture of your driving license," he said and lounged against the doorframe when Aled took the wallet. "It's not good, is it?"

Aled rolled his eyes. "Oh, like yours is better."

"Don't have one."

"Your passport, then."

"Don't have one of those, either."

"What are you, an illegal?"

Gabriel laughed. "Nope. Just don't get around much."

"That's not what I've heard."

Gabriel watched the wallet vanish into a pocket and the blatant lack of movement of Aled's feet. "So — what's my reward?"

"Sorry?"

"For finding it. It feels like reward territory to me."

Aled's eyebrow crawled upwards. "Does it now?"

"Yep."

"Not being funny, but I've known you, what, a day? And I've fucked you more times than I've had different people."

Gabriel's jaw sagged. Seriously? He'd not had three people in his whole life?

"How old are you?"

Aled blinked. "Er. Thirty-three."

"And you've only had three people?"

"I've had five people."

"You've fucked me three times."

"You've had seven orgasms, though. That's sex. So I've fucked you seven times."

Gabriel laughed and caught his wrist. "Oh, I *like* you. You want to give me another one, then?"

He towed Aled into the flat and locked the door firmly behind him. But to his surprise, Aled didn't seize him like he had last time — he simply stepped forward, cupped the back of Gabriel's neck in one broad palm and kissed him.

Just —

Kissed him.

It was soft. Sweet. Gentle.

Loving.

Gabriel's heart skipped a beat. It was the aftercare kiss that Kevin gave him when the scene had been brutal. It was the kisses Jim used to give when he cuddled up at night and thought Gabriel was asleep. It was —

"You okay?" Gabriel murmured.

"Shit evening."

"Want to stay the night?"

Aled coughed a laugh, backing up. He flushed dully. "I, uh. Bad idea."

"Why?"

"I'm — I shouldn't screw when I'm feeling...off."

"Off," Gabriel echoed. He narrowed his eyes. Off. Who shouldn't have sex when they were feeling off? Sex was the best cure for feeling off. Unless —

He smirked.

"Guess you aren't a vanilla accountant after all."

Aled chuckled, rubbing the back of his neck. The slightly embarrassed look was oddly appealing.

"How about you stay anyway?" Gabriel said. "You could thank me by springing for burgers at the place down the road. We could eat, watch TV, watch some porn, whatever."

"That...sounds nice."

Gabriel snorted. "Real charmer, aren't you?"

The answering smile was a little wan, but Aled toed off his shoes and followed Gabriel to the sofa like their sexual preferences were the wrong way round. Gabriel tossed the leaflet for the burger place at him and told him to get ordering, then flopped down onto the cushions, fished out the remote and began to channel surf.

"Do we have to go and get it, or will they deliver?" Aled asked as he hung up and collapsed onto the other half of the sofa.

"They come here," Gabriel said. "I don't really go out in the evenings around here."

"Why not?"

"Not the best career move in the world," Gabriel said.

"Why not move?"

"Council flat. I go where they put me."

Aled made a disgruntled noise of understanding. Gabriel eyed him curiously. His driving license had quoted a Wakefield address, so unless he'd still been in Belle Isle from this morning, he'd shown up far too fast for a bus. He must have a car. And his coat was from a department store, but it could have been a sale.

The tell was his glasses, though. Designer. He'd seen the tiny Gucci stamp on the leg when Aled had been fucking him into next week.

"I'm guessing you rent private," Gabriel said.

"Mortgage."

"Really?"

Aled shrugged. "I'm thirty-three. And my — er. I get a decent salary. And house prices are cheap in Wakefield."

Gabriel was sceptical. Totally on his own? Gabriel was willing to bet that Aled had been about to say that him *and* his wife earned a decent salary. It would explain the grubby, scratched wedding ring.

"Does your wife have a good job, too?"

Aled's fist clenched. The ring gleamed dully. His jaw worked soundlessly for a moment and Gabriel cringed.

"Sorry," he said. "Forget I as —"

"I shouldn't be wearing this anymore."

Gabriel watched silently as Aled worked the ring off his finger. It was tight — probably old — and he dropped it onto the floor with a heavy clang. He flexed his fingers like he'd taken off a ball and chain, but his mouth was still twisted up in the most miserable expression that Gabriel had ever seen.

Oh shit.

Divorced or dead, and Gabriel didn't want to ask. He swallowed, fishing for a solution, and settled right back on humour.

"My ex-boyfriend proposed to me to get us a free meal at a fancy restaurant."

Aled blinked. "What?"

"He took me to this posh place for my twentieth birthday, and —"

"Twentieth?" Aled's jaw sagged. "Sorry, are you — please tell me you're not twenty."

"Twenty-four. Shut up, I'm telling a story."

"You're nine years younger than me."

"So? Anyway, he took me to this flash place — I was still living in Sheffield back then — and we were both dirt poor so I spent the whole time worrying he was going to try and make me run for it, and I didn't want to get arrested, but then just as they brought dessert out, he does a proper down-on-one-knee proposal and they waived the price."

Aled snorted with laughter. "I take it you said yes?"

"For a free meal? Sure."

"So he was your fiancé."

"Only for about half an hour," Gabriel said. "Jim was great, but I'd never have married him. I'm never going to marry anyone. I'm not good at that whole serial monogamy thing."

"Marriage isn't monogamous."

"Uh, yes, it is."

"Not necessarily." The pinched look had faded and Aled slowly sat back, pushing his feet out until they slid under the coffee table. "Me—my wife and I had an open marriage."

Gabriel cocked his head, a smile inching its way onto his face. Aled just got more and more tempting. Could fuck like a machine and didn't get bent out of shape about polyamory?

"I might keep you," Gabriel said, tossing Aled the remote.

"Keep me?"

"Yep. I have regulars."

"Regulars?" Aled snorted with laughter. "What, friends with benefits?"

"Wouldn't really call Michael a *friend*, but yeah, if that's how you want to sleep at night."

"Who's Michael?"

"A knob," Gabriel said, wrinkling his nose. "He's a *great* lay, got a dick that's about a foot long, but he can be a total twat, too."

Aled paused on some science fiction film and put the remote aside. Then he frowned.

"How does he even put his trousers on, with a foot-long dick?"

Gabriel cackled with laughter, the puzzled expression on Aled's face sending him over the edge. Aled smirked slowly, then even more slowly pushed himself up from his seat, and leaned over Gabriel to press him into the cushions and scrape that rough, harsh stubble against his neck.

Gabriel abruptly stopped laughing and groaned instead.

"I do come with a lot of benefits," Aled murmured in his ear. "And I think a bit of you is good for the soul."

"Mm, want to stay the night after all?" Gabriel whispered, closing his eyes as stubble grazed his cheek and ear. *Christ.* If he kept Aled, he was going to break into his house and destroy all his razors.

"Depends…"

"On what?"

"Is there a rental fee for half the bed?"

"Yeah. One orgasm per night."

"Tell you what—" A hand brushed the front of Gabriel's jogging bottoms, and a finger expertly found his already interested dick. "Dinner and a movie, then I'll suck you off again for dessert. That enough to earn me a night?"

Gabriel laughed and twisted his head for a messy kiss. It wasn't the sweet one at the door anymore. It was filth. Aled was obviously feeling better already and Gabriel was completely up for taking advantage.

"That'll earn you a whole week," he said. "But the burgers will be half an hour yet. So why not push the boat out and start with the dessert?"

Chapter Nine

Monday was like waiting for the end of the world.

Aled worked for an international advertising firm. Once, he'd been a graphic designer. Now, he was the head of marketing and the nearest he got to designing anything was choosing how to politically say, "This campaign idea is a load of shit," to the board. On a good day, his job was well-paid but boring. On a bad day, like Monday, it was like expensive torture.

And even the usual Monday afternoon with Suze wasn't going to save it.

Suze and Tom shared a car. And on Mondays, Tom needed it. So Mondays had long been the Aled-and-Suze day, when they'd leave work in his car, head off to the gym for a swimming and spa session together, then he'd run her home in time for tea. Usually, the perfect antidote to having not won the weekend lottery yet again and — in Suze's case — a reward for not having murdered Ann, her boss in the HR division.

But not that Monday.

Not with the divorce papers haunting his fingers and the sharp pain of isolation crackling along his skin ever since his Saturday fuck with a stranger.

"Right," Suze said, slamming the passenger door and kicking off her high heels. "Step on it. I need a swim, then I need a long, *long* soak in the hydrotherapy pool, whilst imagining drowning Ann in it. God, that woman can make a meeting out of an email, I swear. Then you can tell me why you've been such a grumpy—"

"Melissa wants a divorce."

Silence.

Then, *"Oh."*

More silence.

Then an "Oh, Aled, sweetheart," and Suze's arms were around his shoulders. Aled swallowed thickly, clenching his hands numbly around the steering wheel, then removed the key from the ignition and sat back.

"She wants a divorce," he croaked, "and I responded by going round to the flat of a guy I meet on a sleazy sex website and sucking him off like I'd hired him for the job."

"Oh, love."

"She wants a fucking *divorce*, Suze."

Then his voice cracked and the tears spilled over. Suze made a crooning noise, then his face was pulled into her neck, her soft hair surrounding him, and he latched on and cried. Suddenly, he wasn't a thirty-three-year-old marketing executive with a flash car and a cheap suit. He was a heartbroken kid again, crying on his best friend's shoulder because, somehow, the girl he was in love with had walked away, and the girl he wasn't had stayed.

"Why couldn't I have bloody well married *you?*" he croaked miserably as the crying jag eased and Suze kissed his ear before peeling herself free and supplying him with a liberal amount of tissues.

"Because the sex would be crazy weird."

He laughed wetly and Suze gave him her sweetest, most sympathetic smile.

"I am sorry, sweetheart," she said softly, "but you must know it's for the best."

"How is getting *divorced* going to fix anything?"

Suze sighed. "Because there's no fixing this. Melissa's not some—some silly brain-dead harpy you can win back with a few vague promises and a bunch of flowers. You knew when she left that she probably wasn't coming back."

"I thought—the *time*, Suze, I thought she just needed time, that maybe—"

Suze rubbed his arm. "I'm sorry, love, I really am. I'm so sorry. But you know, you've always known, that she wasn't likely to be back."

It was a sharp stab in the ears. And Aled fought to keep himself from crying again. "I still fucking *hoped*," he breathed.

"It's for the best."

"How? What, admitting I fucked up and lost her, and—"

"Yes."

The word was sharp and it brought Aled up short.

"Yes, Aled. Admit it. You lost her. She's gone. Until you admit that, you're *never* going to move on, and, sweetheart, you've been—God, you've not been well for months. And you *need* to let go of her. If it takes a divorce to do it, maybe it's for the best."

"I always...I thought she'd come back. I thought maybe she'd—I don't know, she'd remember that other guys are shits and she went for the goofy-looking ginger for a reason—"

"She went for you," Suze said quietly, "because you're an amazing, loving man and she could see it. And I can see it, and Tom sees it, and you are chipping away at yourself this last year, just—what, waiting for her? Stop waiting, Aled. Let her go and find someone else, find someone who wants the same things you do."

"I want her."

Suze's fingers ghosted over his arm in the lightest of touches. "Sometimes, we don't get what we want."

Aled closed his eyes. That was the cruellest part. The final straw, the thing that had broken their marriage and sent Melissa out of the door—it wasn't his fault. And it wasn't her fault. It was just one of those things. One of those things that could break couples, right down the middle, and *had* broken them.

But Aled couldn't explain why. They could have worked around it, maybe. If he'd known she was going to walk out, say nothing for a year, then send him divorce papers, he would have given in and worked around it. He wouldn't have said no. He would have said, "Let's try it another way."

He said as much and Suze sighed.

"And you would have ended up resenting her," she said softly, "for saddling you with a life you didn't want. And if you'd not, and she'd have come back, she would have resented you for taking away the life she *did* want."

"I could have—"

"Done nothing. Sweetheart, there was no way you were going to solve that one. And anyway, even if you had, it wasn't the only issue. She didn't like you and me, you never convinced her we're not a thing and she wasn't too thrilled about the whole cock-coveting thing."

Aled coughed a wet laugh, scrubbing his wrist across his eyes. "Coveting cock? What the hell, Suze?"

"I've seen you eyeing up that guy in security, you covet his cock plenty."

"I covet his *arse*, thank you, it's a nice arse."

Then the brief levity crumpled and Aled took a shaky breath.

"God, Suze, my wife wants to divorce me and I went round to a stranger's flat and blew him instead of – of talking to her, calling her, sorting it out, working it out—"

"You've not really tried to do any of that since she left," Suze said softly. "She walked and you wallowed. Time to face the music, love. I'm sorry, but you will both be better off if you let her go. You can both move on. Maybe you could even be friends again one day."

Aled snorted.

"And on the subject of moving on, did you visit a prostitute? Because that was not what I had in mi—"

"No," Aled interrupted with a wan smile. "No, he's not a prostitute. Probably. I mean, I didn't pay him and, really, if anyone would have been charging fees on Saturday it should have been me—"

"What are you talking about?"

"Gabriel."

"Who?"

"Gabriel. The guy Tom set me up with on Grindr."

Suze blinked, then laughed a little. "Wait, Tom actually *did* that? I thought you two were just drunk and kidding!"

"No, he did it. Well, I sent the message. We met up the next morning and fucked a couple of times, then I—

I went back that evening, after Melissa gave me the divorce papers, and I just—we got burgers and watched TV and I sucked him off until he was shaking like a smack addict in withdrawal."

"Did he like it?"

And that right there was why Suze was his best friend. Even Tom would grimace at the phrase. Suze just went for the interrogation.

"Yeah."

"So—your response to your wife asking for a divorce was to go *back* to the one-night stand you'd only left that morning and do him again?"

"I guess so."

Suze laughed, the sound actually infectious, and Aled found himself cracking a very thin smile. "Oh my God, Aled. And you're still saying you want to get Melissa back? Come on, sweetie. You're carrying on with this guy—"

"One day doesn't equate to carrying on."

"You went back—it's not a one-night stand anymore."

"I didn't have anyone else to fuck, and—shit, Suze, he makes you feel so fucking good. I needed that. I needed to feel good for once."

Suze's face softened. "See what I mean when I say you've not been well?"

Aled closed his eyes again, the pain sharp and burning in his chest.

"Sweetheart. Sign the papers. Let her go. And get *better*, okay?"

"Doing what? Fucking random people off dodgy websites? Going home to my empty house? Knowing that—that the woman I love more than I've ever loved anyone is fucking some other guy, having his kids and wearing his wedding ring?"

"Aled—"

"It's just a shag, Suze, and yeah, it made me feel better, but it made me feel fucking lonely, too. I haven't—a whole year and there's been nobody, a whole fucking *year* while she's been out moving on, and—"

"And you can't blame Melissa for that. You're the one who's wallowed, Aled. She told you it was over and you've not moved an inch since."

"Where am I supposed to move *to*?"

"To having fun again! To meeting people again! Yeah, maybe Tom's right, maybe some meaningless sex is a good way to shake her out of your mind a little bit, but you need to try dating again sometime, too. So you and Melissa didn't work out. And you know what, *so* what. She was your first serious relationship and it was never perfect, you can't claim it was perfect—"

"It *was* perfect."

"Don't be stupid," Suze said harshly. "She thought you were knocking off your best mate and was jealous as hell about me. She never *really* believed you were bisexual and got annoyed if you commented on blokes. You hated one of her colleagues for fancying her like mad, even though you were supposedly all open, even after you got married. You never got the bathroom refitted because you argued so much about the design. And that's before we even get to the big one, the fact she wanted—"

"I get it, Suze, thanks," Aled said sharply. "All right, fine, it wasn't perfect, but it was perfect for *me*. It was what I wanted! All I wanted! And I just—I just want my fucking wife back, Suze, I want my wife back, I want her back, I want — "

The tears dissolved his vision and Suze's hair surrounded his world again, her grip firm and unyielding even as she scolded him for his denial and said he ought to be seeing a counsellor, getting some kind of help, where was trying to get back a woman who wanted to divorce him ever going to get him, he needed to focus on his Grindr account and the instructor at the gym who fancied him, not Melissa and their never-finished bathroom...

"Just sign the papers, sweetheart, and end this mess. *Please.*"

"I can't."

He couldn't do it. He couldn't just give up, give in, let go. He couldn't. He *couldn't.*

"I can't do it, Suze."

Because if he did, what in the hell was he supposed to do to replace it? He didn't want to date and he didn't know how to. He'd never dated. He'd met Melissa when he was a teenager and they'd been together ever since. How *did* adults meet? Where was he supposed to find another woman, never mind another man?

"Do you mind if I just drop you at home?" he found himself asking. "I just — I can't face it today. I want to just go home."

"Aled — "

"Please."

She wavered. He could see it in her face. The indecision, the anxiety, the edges of anger. He knew her expressions better than he knew his own — but for once, he didn't care. Let her be angry. Let her be worried. He just wanted to go *home.*

"Okay."

She offered three times on the way to hers to come over to his, but Aled just shook his head. He didn't want her to. He didn't want to hear how Melissa asking for a divorce was a good thing. Pathetic as it was, he wanted to drink the house dry, go through their photos and wonder if it wouldn't have been less brutal, less awful, if Melissa had died. Dead people didn't *want* to leave you. Dead people didn't choose to go. Divorced wives did.

But the house, when he got home, was disapproving.

It wasn't *his* house, in a way. They'd lived here. Their first home. Aled had paid the mortgage — Melissa had still been studying, with no money to her name — but it had been theirs. The kitchen was all hers. The garden, with all her favourite plants. She'd bought him exercise equipment and a weights bench that had been rotting in the garage ever since, to combat his soft edges and spare tyre. He'd used them every January, intent on a new regime, and never stuck to it. God, even the curtains framing the conservatory doors had Melissa all over them — she'd repaired the hems when they'd frayed the winter that the boiler needed replacing and they didn't have the money for things like curtains.

It was *theirs.*

Only she wasn't here and never wanted to come back. So it was empty and cold. It was like renting a furnished flat. Hostile. Alien. Someone else's décor. It was quiet. No radio, no singing from the bathroom. Her shoes hadn't been kicked off at the bottom of the stairs and her jumper didn't decorate the back of the sofa anymore.

Aled swallowed, his throat heavy, and raked both hands through his hair. He couldn't do this. He couldn't just sit drinking in this empty house, thinking of the wife who didn't want him anymore. He had to…do something else. Get out, get someone else in, *do* something. Or he would just drink himself blind and feel shit for it anyway and prove Suze right. He just —

His phone buzzed in his pocket.

Sliding it out, he saw it was just another text from Sky, reminding him of his due bill, but Aled clicked out of it and scrolled to find Gabriel. So what if it was just a fuck? He needed — something. He needed a fuck, or at least a friend. A friend who didn't know her, who couldn't and wouldn't comment on it or offer advice. A friend who could take his mind off her completely, and none of Aled's friends could do that. All of them — every last one — predated the night she left. All of them knew her.

Many had walked *with* her.

So maybe it wasn't healthy, maybe it was just as stupid as reacting to a divorce pack by fucking someone else, but — fuck it, Aled *needed* someone else right now. He needed to not just be the sad bastard left behind for something he couldn't help, needed to feel good again, just for a minute, and Gabriel had made him feel so good —

Me: Free to come over tonight? I can offer the finest takeaway menus in Wakefield and a bit of fun.

He *could* offer home cooking, technically, but he'd never been that good at it. And he could maybe break out the wine instead of the beer — Gabriel didn't strike him as a beer drinker, despite his tiny flat in a crappy part of Leeds.

Gabriel Grindr: Sorry, got plans tonight. Another time though? Can you offer another brick wall? ;) x

Aled swallowed and closed his eyes, the disappointment washing over him in a wave. His stomach tightened and he felt oddly angry with himself, even as he thumbed out a bland *no worries.* His eyes burned. God, why was he fucking upset? They'd just shagged a couple of times. Of course Gabriel had other plans. They'd met only a couple of *days* ago. How clingy could Aled bloody well be? It wasn't like they were bloody dating. It wasn't like —

Aled cut his own thoughts off and put the phone aside, his stomach churning and his heart hurting. *Fuck it.* Fuck Tom's warnings about his imminent alcohol problem and fuck Suze's insistence that he sign the papers. He didn't want to think. He didn't want to feel. And so what if it all hit him tomorrow? He could deal with that *tomorrow.*

He was going to get absolutely wankered and he was going to look at the photos of his *wife,* of the woman he *loved,* and pretend it hadn't all gone so bloody wrong.

Chapter Ten

Gabriel's breath hitched as the hot flood of cum caught him by surprise. He clenched, dragging the pleasure out, closing his eyes and gasping through the feel of it, digging his fingers into the sheets and heaving for air. Fuck, he loved this. This feeling of being split open and filled, this feeling like he was nothing more than an attractive body and had no purpose but to be fucked.

God, it felt good.

His mouth was captured and Gabriel sighed into the hungry kiss, then nudged his face aside and laughed. "Shower," he whispered, his voice hoarse from shouting, and was kissed again.

"I have to go soon."

"Then fuck *in* the shower and you can go," Gabriel bargained.

The man pulled out, too sudden and too soon, and Gabriel clenched around the empty space he left behind. He reached, but the man was already climbing off the bed, sweat glistening in the light from the bedside lamp.

"Can't. I really do have to go."

"Wife calling?"

The guy coloured faintly. "I'm not married," he said, but Gabriel had seen the pale strip of skin on his ring finger. Gabriel shrugged.

"Not my problem if you are. Just want to know if calling you again would be a bad idea."

The man grinned, coming back to bite his bottom lip and kiss him. "It would be a *very* good idea," he said, stroking his palm up Gabriel's bare thigh. "I'm quite busy, but I'll send you a message."

"If it's a very good idea," Gabriel bargained, reaching for that soft cock and cupping it in one hand, "then you could stay for another round."

The man laughed and shook his head, pulling away. "Even if I had the time," he said, reaching for his underwear, "I'm not bloody twenty-five. I can't get it up again that fast."

Gabriel laughed, spreading his legs wider and playing idly with himself. "Ah, the affliction of the cisgender man."

The man frowned. "You what?"

Gabriel rolled his eyes. "Never mind. Help yourself to the kitchen. I just have to shower."

The man slapped his arse as Gabriel clambered free of the messy bed, but made no further attempt, and Gabriel slipped into the bathroom with mixed feelings. Gorgeous, certainly. Perhaps he would call the man again for a second go. But he wouldn't be selling his soul for that — the sex had been good but somewhat unimaginative. Clothes off, cock in arse — he hadn't even *considered* the cunt — and a dull rhythm. The man had obviously learned to fuck at the school of drunken parties. And was obviously trying a sexuality on for size.

Gabriel tipped his head back under the water and slowly began to toy with himself again. The guy had gotten Gabriel off first, though, and that earned big points in Gabriel's book. He liked a good fuck, but at the end of the day, it would take a bloody hour of being fucked raw before he came on cock alone. He might be able to get off several times in a row but having been assigned female did hinder matters slightly when it came to anal.

When the last of the evidence had been washed away — aside from a clean bruise on Gabriel's hip that made him smile — Gabriel stepped out and rubbed down with a hand towel before slipping back into the rest of the flat, completely naked and still damp. Temptation on two legs and he knew it.

Only, to his disappointment, to find himself alone.

"I guess soon meant *soon*," he muttered to himself and rummaged up his phone from the kitchenette. He had a couple of new messages and another unsolicited dick pic — albeit an impressively big one, it did have to be said — but nothing of much interest. And he could do with another, really. The man had taken the edge off, but Gabriel had just had his shot yesterday and the week after his shot he *always* wanted to fuck until it hurt to sit.

Shrugging, he retreated to the bedroom to strip the sheets and change the bed, then he could get the bus into town and scour the clubs, perhaps. He never pulled direct from them — the lure was dangerous and the risk of someone being a little too surprised by not getting the penis they expected was too high — but passing out his Grindr profile always worked. He could line up a few guys for tomorrow, or —

Gabriel stopped dead in the bedroom doorway, staring at the bedside table.

And the cash folded and tucked under the base of the lamp.

Money.

The fucker had left him *money*.

"You fucking bastard!" Gabriel exploded, snatching up the cash and counting even as he dialled. When it connected, he didn't pause. "You fucking cunt! I'm not some fucking hooker, you cheating piece of shit! You think flashing a hundred at me will get me grabbing my ankles and moaning like a whore for you, or do you pay your fucking wife a handful of twenties to get her to open her legs, too?"

The man spluttered some kind of protest, something about hook-up sites and figuring out his sexuality and Gabriel looking like he needed the money, and Gabriel swore viciously at him again.

"If you ever so much as *think* about contacting me again, I'll find you and I'll find that wife you apparently don't have and I'll make *sure* she knows you're fucking trans men because you're not quite gay enough for the so-called real thing, you son of a bitch!"

Gabriel heard perhaps half a swear in reply before he drew his hand back and flung the phone at the wall. It smashed to pieces, glass and plastic exploding over the dressing table, and for a moment, he simply stood and breathed, eyes closed and the anger pulsing in time with his heart. Fuck's sake, wasn't he fucking *allowed* to enjoy sex? Was there some code he'd missed, where if a trans guy was offering a shag, it really meant he wanted paying for it? Obviously, there was no fucking way Gabriel *enjoyed* sex, not being trans and living in a dodgy area. No, clearly he was a professional prostitute.

Exhaling, and deflating, Gabriel sat heavily on the edge of the bed and raked his fingers through his hair. Fuck the clubs. He'd probably just find some other closeted bellend who figured it wasn't gay if the guy he was screwing — in the *arse,* no less — still had his original plumbing. Clearly it wasn't gay if you were within twenty feet of vagina at the time, Gabriel thought bitterly. He didn't need more like that. More cis guys who told themselves they were open-minded when really, in their heads, he was just a woman with small tits.

No, he needed to get it from a trusted source, from someone who knew what he liked, knew what Gabriel was and didn't offer pathetic cover stories and fucking *money* for the privilege.

Gabriel glanced at the ruin of the phone and nodded to himself. Aled. Aled ticked those boxes and he'd asked earlier.

Rescuing the SIM card from the remains, Gabriel retreated to the kitchenette, found a spare handset in one of the drawers, plugged the SIM in and scrolled quickly to Aled's name.

Me: Change of plans. Still offering those fine takeaways and a wall?

Maybe he could provoke a bit of that slamming-against-objects again. Maybe he could persuade Aled to go easy on the lube this time, and screw away the married man who thought he could figure out his sexuality by paying someone like Gabriel to open his legs.

Aled: Still offering. Where are you?

Me: Home.

Aled: Can't drive, train will take forever and you'll still have to walk it. Get a taxi to mine.

Gabriel snorted, thinking of the money on the table. Wouldn't that be precious, the man's hundred quid going to get Gabriel a proper fuck from a proper man.

Me: That'll cost a bomb.

Aled: I'll cover it, it's fine.

Me: Nah, I got it.

Might as well put that bloody fuck-money to good use.

Me: This cocksucker just left me money for it like I'm some kind of hooker. I'll spend it on getting me to a real man.

Aled: What an arse. Who needs to pay to get laid anyway?

Me: Guys who think screwing me still lets them be straight because they're within twenty feet of vagina?

Aled: Tosser.

Aled: I'd want my money back if I'd paid for a girl and got you.

Aled: Did he tip?

Gabriel grinned. God, he *liked* Aled. The guy might look meek and harmless, but he definitely wasn't.

Then he sent a postcode, a house number and an offer of scented lube. Gabriel smirked and sent one last message before calling for a taxi.

Me: On my way. And go easy on the lube. I want it harder this time.

* * * *

Aled lived on the Darnley estate, as it turned out.

The address got Gabriel dropped off on one of the larger roads in the estate. The house itself was kind of nice-looking, with dark brickwork and painted wooden windows, a garage and suspiciously clean 4x4 on the driveway off to one side. It smacked of first home, to Gabriel—either that, or Aled was such a petrolhead that he'd spend thirty grand on a car but not a hundred grand on a house.

Still, it was a massive step up from a one-bed council flat in Belle Isle, Gabriel thought as he picked his way up the narrow path and rang the bell. And Aled had mentioned an ex he'd been with for ages. Maybe he'd once lived in a proper fancy house, the type of house that people who owned suspiciously clean 4x4s would have, but they had to split the house and Aled had ended up here?

Definitely that, Gabriel decided, when Aled opened the door, dressed in obviously tailored suit trousers and a pale blue dress shirt, the effect mildly lost by the mismatched socks on his shoe-free feet.

Gabriel grinned and nodded to the car. "That looks like you can drive."

"This looks like I can't," Aled retorted and held up a half-full wine glass.

Gabriel froze.

Shit. *Shit!* Of course. Of *course* that was what Aled had meant. He was in his fucking thirties and had like five credit cards and a goddamned driving license in his wallet. Of *course* he could drive normally. How could Gabriel have been so —

"It's just Echo Falls, but it's nice," Aled was saying blithely and Gabriel felt his chest seize in something like panic when Aled held out the glass. "Try it. I just cracked the bottle open so I'll pour you a glass if you want."

Gabriel wanted it. He *always* wanted it. He always *would.* It would be so easy just to take it, just smile and say it was nice and take it, Aled would never have to know, nobody had to —

"Gabriel?" The glass was lowered. "You all right?"

Gabriel took a deep breath. "I — I can't drink."

"Oh, sorry. Some sort of medical thing I should know about? I mean, I'm guessing from the other night it's not a religious issue — "

Gabriel shook his head, finally tearing his gaze away from the glass. "No, it's — I was, I *am,* an alcoholic. Three years sober." And he'd counted every damn day of them. "I can't drink. At all. I can't even kiss someone who's had something strong."

Aled blinked, then swore. "Shit, I'm so sorry, I had no idea. I'll just — well, come in, don't just stand on my doorstep…"

Gabriel inched over the threshold, folding his arms around himself, and Aled shut the door, then disappeared into a tiny kitchen off to the left. Gabriel heard a fridge door close, then Aled brushed past him again.

"Give me half a minute," he said, disappearing up some stairs on Gabriel's right. "Make yourself at home, except in the fridge!" he shouted back down and Gabriel hesitantly went for the only other option – forward.

The living room dominated the house, a tasteful and surprisingly neat room that was basically monochromatic – white walls, cream carpet and black furniture – but with dark red cushions splashing a little life into things. A small conservatory lay beyond, lit by lights designed to look like candles, and the shadow of a garden fence and the side of what Gabriel presumed to be the garage lurked beyond the windows. A couple of framed photographs hung on the walls – an old wedding photograph of a ginger-haired groom and an Indian bride, a holiday photo of Aled and a pretty woman with reddish-blonde hair on some skiing trip, both beaming stupidly beneath absurdly large ski masks and, rather strangely, one of a dark-haired man pushing a blonde woman with bright green wellies in a wheelbarrow at some country fair.

It was a nice house, Gabriel decided, and slowly unglued his hands from his elbows in favour of exploring. Aled kept a lot of DVDs and Gabriel was amused to notice several porn films amongst the collection, filed shamelessly between superhero movies and slushy romances. He didn't seem to be much of a reader, although he *did* have several photo albums in a bookshelf beside a ridiculously large TV and he was a tech geek – the coffee table held a laptop, a tablet and two smartphones – albeit one literally labelled *work* and switched off — and there was a desktop computer set up on a large wooden desk across the room with two screens and a stack of external hard drives.

Yeah, Gabriel had hit this guy bang on the nose. *Geek.*

"Sorry." He jumped when Aled reappeared in the living room doorway. "Teeth brushed, mouth washed out, wine stashed away and a new offering — Sprite?"

Gabriel laughed, a little touched by the consideration, and took the offered wine glass of lemonade. "You didn't have to —" he started, but Aled shook his head.

"Yeah, I did, if you can't even kiss someone who's been drinking."

"You could have just not kissed me."

Aled raised his eyebrows, then leaned in and planted a firm kiss on Gabriel's mouth. It was chaste and brief, but the intent very clear and Gabriel had to blink a couple of times to gather his wits.

"No way," Aled said. "I have a thing for lips and honestly, it was your smile on your profile that made me message you. I'm a sucker for a nice smile."

Gabriel ducked his head, grinning sheepishly, and Aled laughed.

"That's the one. Anyway, it's fine. I'm not a huge drinker myself unless Suze is involved. I'll just remember not to invite you over if I've been out with her."

"Who's Suze?"

"Best mate," Aled said and gestured to the picture of the woman in the wheelbarrow. "Bad influence, she'd only tell you horrible stories about me. So, are you any good at cooking?"

Gabriel blinked, the sudden change in subject startling. "Um, well, yeah, I guess. You know, microwave meals for one, my speciality."

Aled laughed again. "God, thanks for coming over," he said in a rush that sounded like a confession. "It's been a shitty couple of days, I needed a pick-me-up."

"You could have skipped the small talk and gone straight for the picking up, you know, I'm hardly skittish," Gabriel teased, making to set the glass aside. It would pick *him* up, too, and push out that wanker from earlier. Aled didn't try to leave him money like he was a bloody fuck-for-hire.

"Ah, no, you're good company with your clothes on, too. I was thinking, seeing as how I've ruined any attempt I'd made at a lasagne, I could call for a takeaway, and we could try making dessert ourselves, *then* maybe have the pick-me-up?"

"It'll be late by then…"

Aled stepped right into Gabriel's space and kissed him. Distinctly not chastely. His lips were warm and smooth, and he tasted of spearmint, overpoweringly strong. He kissed as though he were exploring, moving slowly over Gabriel's lips before pushing in farther and almost stroking Gabriel's mouth, one hand coming up to cup the back of Gabriel's head.

Gabriel slowly pulled himself free, resting his forehead against Aled's and trying to remember how to talk and breathe at the same time. Finally, he managed, "Um…I guess I could stay the night."

Aled beamed. "Do you like Italian food?"

"It'll do."

It felt scarily date-like, even though the fancy restaurant was actually Aled's tiny kitchen and porn-hub of a living room, but the strange feeling subsided after Aled had called whatever the place was for their food and turned out all the cupboards for dessert ingredients. He admitted the only dessert he knew was his grandmother's cookie recipe—"You're not diabetic or anything, right? These'll kill you if you're diabetic"—but after Gabriel admitted he knew half a brownie recipe, they opted to combine the two and, if they sucked, pass them off on the finance department at Aled's office.

Turned out, Gabriel *could* cook better than Aled. Miraculously, the man didn't even know how to knead dough, and when Gabriel demonstrated, he had his fingers peeled off the finished dough before he could begin to cut it, was backed into the fridge, and his index finger sucked into Aled's mouth.

"That's not like cake mix."

Aled pulled off with a grimace. "No shit. Way too much flour."

"We could always google how to make cake if you want to lick cake mix off me," Gabriel offered a little breathlessly as Aled tried another, less floury finger. That was met with the same face.

"I think we should. This is only sexy for you."

"Yeah, it's pretty sexy for me. Except for the bit where you have flour on your face," Gabriel added.

"I do not," Aled said, checking in the back of a spoon, so Gabriel rectified the situation, picking up a handful of it from the counter and literally throwing it.

For a split second, Aled froze, staring at him.

"You—"

Gabriel laughed. "You look ridiculous."

Aled's answer was twofold. Firstly, he emptied the remains of the flour bag over Gabriel's head. And secondly, he knocked Gabriel's legs out from under him and took them both crashing to the floor, where he pinned Gabriel with his heavier weight and planted Gabriel's own dough-caked hand on his face.

"Eurgh, oh my God!"

They wrestled in the mess, Gabriel fighting to put his hands in Aled's fiery hair, somehow still ginger despite the rest of him looking like a cocaine factory had exploded on him, before Aled seized Gabriel's head in both hands, leaned down and kissed him.

Gabriel stilled and relaxed his jaw. This kiss was nothing like the other kisses. This kiss was insistent and domineering. This kiss didn't explore him or make a point—it forced him open and held him still. Aled's erection was against Gabriel's thigh and the way his weight was bearing down on Gabriel's hips kept him trapped. Gabriel rolled his hips up, opening his legs and gathering Aled into him, hooking an ankle over Aled's calf and swallowing the muted groan that resulted.

"That's dirty pool," Aled whispered, leaving Gabriel's mouth in favour of his neck, burying his teeth there and biting. Gabriel gasped, arching up into the thrill, his heart suddenly pounding, and shivered. "Interesting," Aled murmured. "If I bit you enough, would you come?"

Gabriel groaned as he did it again. "Probably," he whispered. "I mean, you could always put your hand down my jeans and help it along a little."

Aled bit him again, much harder this time, and Gabriel shuddered, hitching his leg higher and grinding himself against Aled's thigh. He was getting wet. If Aled bit him again, he'd be able to just pull Gabriel's jeans down and fuck him right there on the kitchen floor, as long as he hadn't managed to roll his cock in flour.

"Do it," Gabriel said breathlessly, guiding one of Aled's hands to his fly. "I'm nearly there already. Just get inside me and make me *really* messy."

"What, flour in all your hair?" Aled quipped, then he was suddenly gone, sinking down Gabriel's body and ripping his jeans down like they were on fire.

"Where are you—*fuck!*" Gabriel yelped, as Aled's tongue rubbed itself, hot and rough, right up from his arse to his bellybutton a thick, wet, floury stripe. Then that mouth latched on to his cock and began to massage it between Aled's lips, leaving Gabriel a shuddering mess on the floor, biting down on his own forearm to stop himself yelling the place down, and his knees pinned apart by Aled's firm grip. *Oh God, and what a grip.* He had hands like steel—he could force Gabriel's legs open if he wanted, just push him down anywhere, any time and open his legs as though Gabriel were his own personal fleshlight with a pulse. He was almost biting down there, the nips hard enough to graze and warn, but light enough that they were thrilling, exciting, so damn fucking *good* –

The doorbell rang.

"You are fucking *kidding* me!" Gabriel spat and Aled laughed, blowing gently over him and crawling up his body again to kiss him roughly on the mouth.

"Stay right there," he said, then wiped his mouth off on his sleeve and got up. Gabriel lay stunned, blinking at the ceiling, just lying on Aled's kitchen floor, covered in flour with his jeans and briefs around his ankles and his orgasm about thirty seconds away before it had been interrupted by a delivery boy. He scowled and hauled himself up, kicking off his jeans entirely and briefly considering the briefs before losing them, too.

His packer had stayed in them, but was floured to death. Great. Just—

The front door slammed and Aled reappeared. He frowned. "I told you to stay right there."

"After you left me in the middle of a tongue fuck?"

"Not very good at taking orders, are you?" Aled asked and slapped Gabriel's bare arse. Hard. The crack and sudden sting made Gabriel groan and he shoved Aled against the oven, fisting both hands in his hair.

"Did we both get pasta?"

"Yes."

"It'll reheat. Finish what you started."

Aled raised his eyebrows, abandoned the bag on the counter and crowded Gabriel back into the fridge, holding both his hands above his head. "You threw the first handful," he challenged and Gabriel rubbed up against the hard-on pressed into his thigh.

"You were tongue-fucking me," he said breathlessly. "Thirty seconds and I'd have come on your face. You owe me. Cock. In. Now."

Aled laughed, dropping Gabriel's hands to tear at his floury trousers and dropping them. He wasn't even *wearing* underwear, and Gabriel got both hands instantly on that rock-hard cock, smearing flour into the pre-cum like a paste. Aled swore, batted them off then seized Gabriel's knees in those insane hands and lifted him up against the fridge.

"Best be ready," he grunted and thrust.

"OhmyfuckingGod."

In one swift movement, Aled was completely inside him. He was hard as iron, just shoving his way in like he owned the place. Then he began to thrust, the power of it pushing Gabriel up and down the fridge. Gabriel locked his legs around Aled's waist and dropped his weight, forcing that cock even deeper, rubbing his own dick against Aled's stomach and snatching at his mouth in a hungry kiss, tasting himself over the flour, smelling his own sex from the attempt on the floor.

"Holy fuck, do it, do it, fuck me, fuck me so hard that I taste salt in the back of my throat, shove it so deep it leaks out when you put me down, *fuck* me, Christ—" Gabriel babbled, burying his face in Aled's hair and thrusting haphazardly back, trying to get more friction and more cock at all once, fisting his dough-covered fingers in the back of Aled's shirt and near-tearing it, hearing the contents of the fridge rattling at his back, the fridge itself barely able to support the movement.

Aled came suddenly, hot liquid flooding Gabriel's insides and the rhythm stuttering and halting as Aled groaned and bit down on Gabriel's neck again, staying buried deep inside him as he rode it out. Gabriel clenched around him, trying to match every pulse with a squeeze, and got a breathless curse for it, before they were sinking to the floor in a tangle, Aled pulling out before Gabriel could tell him to stay, and—

"Oh my God, you have to be kidding me," Gabriel whimpered as Aled wrapped his lips back around Gabriel's short length and *sucked*. He sucked so hard that sensation exploded up Gabriel's limbs and destroyed his nervous system. He lay whimpering and helpless on the filthy tiles, trying to clench his thighs around Aled's head, trying to thrust himself against his teeth and tongue, but able only to lie there and cry as Aled's teeth touched him one last time and Gabriel came so hard that it felt like a seizure, a blackout, a death and a rebirth all at once.

Then he was lying there, naked from the waist down, covered in flour smeared into paste by cum and spit.

"You're a mess. You'll leak all the way up to the bathroom."

Gabriel laughed giddily, his air all gone. "S'your problem."

Aled paused.

Then hands pushed Gabriel's knees even farther apart and Aled's tongue began to clean away all evidence of the fuck.

Chapter Eleven

Aled piled the dishes in the sink and braced himself against the counter.

It was nearly midnight. The kitchen was still a mess, cum and flour all over the floor, and all their clothes were in the wash. They had both had to shower thoroughly, ruining a couple of towels, and Aled had loaned Gabriel a pair of boxers and a sleep shirt.

Which meant Gabriel was, right now, lying in Aled's bed, smelling of Aled's shower gel, wearing Aled's underwear. And was, from the maths Aled was doing, quite possibly into kink.

Aled's dick had done the same maths and didn't care if Aled was tired and it had gotten off once already tonight. It wanted out of his pyjamas and into Gabriel's body. Now. And Aled wanted to let it.

But if Gabriel were a submissive as well…

God, it would be perfect. Imagine that fuckable mouth around a gag. Imagine putting a spreader between those knees and holding him open for hours on end. Imagine grabbing him by the hair and forcing his head down onto Aled's cock. Imagine him wearing a collar, chained to the floor by the bed and opening his legs the minute Aled walked into a room.

Imagine him asking Aled to do it.

Because Aled knew what he'd seen — he just didn't know if *Gabriel knew* it. Not everybody knew anything about BDSM. Most people thought it was all nipple clamps and floggers. Gabriel might not even know what he was, but then…could Aled introduce him to some of it? He wasn't any kind of formal part of the community. He and Melissa had worked out what their preferences and fetishes were from the internet, not from other dominants or kinky couples or anyone like that. They'd just experimented, over and over and over again, until they found their things.

Could he do it again, with Gabriel?

Slowly, as though he were walking through treacle, Aled found the ice cream he'd come down to fetch and doled it out into a couple of bowls. At the very least, he thought, he could probably push for a little bit of kink, a *little* bit, even if Gabriel was wholly ignorant of BDSM play. Most guys — or girls, for that matter — didn't like flour fights ending in sex of any kind in the middle of the kitchen floor, making flour paste out of body fluids. And most people, in Aled's experience, were pretty happy to get pushed up against walls and other objects for a clumsy shag, but didn't start running at the mouth begging to fucked so deep that they'd be able to taste it when they came.

And Gabriel had.

Therefore, vanilla — aside from the ice cream — might not form part of the menu after all.

Armed with ice cream and questions, Aled headed back up the stairs. Gabriel looked pretty, but not exceptionally fuckable, when Aled stepped into the bedroom. He was sitting cross-legged against the pillows, working out the remote control. His hair was spiky and wet from the shower, and Aled's boxers and T-shirt too loose on him. The T-shirt betrayed the faintest outline of his tits, small breasts that Aled had seen but never touched, and his bare feet — which Aled had never paid attention to — looked almost delicate, frail ankles topping high, refined arches. He looked almost ethereal, thin and strange in the bed more used to fat ginger blokes.

Aled said so and Gabriel laughed at him. "Oh, please," he said. "You're stocky, yeah, but you're not fat."

"I'll do a Shatner. I'll be fat by the time I'm fifty."

"Who's Shatner?"

"Dear God, get out," Aled moaned but handed Gabriel his ice cream and slid into bed. Gabriel wriggled up until their thighs pressed together. "Gabe?"

" —riel."

"What?"

"Gabriel."

"Sorry. Fine. Gabriel?"

Gabriel smirked around the spoon. "What?"

Aled thoughtfully prodded his ice cream, wondering the best way to ask, then decided to go for broke. "Are you kinky at all?"

"What do you mean?"

Aled blew upwards into his hair. "You know, like…BDSM, fetishes, anything like that?"

Gabriel paused. For a long moment, only the DVD root menu warbled in the otherwise silent bedroom. Then, eventually, he said, "What makes you say that."

The tone was so flat that it almost didn't count as a question.

Aled bit his lip. "Well…that first time, when I pushed you against the fence, you seemed to like that. And when I told you to behave yourself, and tonight when I said you weren't very good at obeying orders. And you practically attacked me after I smacked your arse. And the way you started talking when you were close, it sounded…well, it seems like you might have a few submissive tendencies."

"A few."

The admission was quiet and Aled barely caught it.

"With the right person," Gabriel said slowly, "I do like playing…those types of games. I have fantasies. But it has to be the right person."

"Could I be the right person?" Aled dared.

"I don't really know you."

"So that's a…not right now, but maybe?"

Gabriel smiled. "Maybe, yes."

"So have you played games before?"

"Yes."

"What kind?"

"Lots of kinds," Gabriel said warily. "No offence, Aled, but some of my fantasies are pretty…extreme. And some guys might take them as an excuse to do things I don't like and tell me I want it because of those fantasies."

Rape fantasies, Aled thought. Or something similar, like kidnapping fantasies or prostitution games. Melissa had rape fantasies. And Aled, truth be told, found them hot as hell to act out, once he trusted his submissive partner not to let it become real.

"Okay, I get it," he said easily. "Have you ever had bad experiences?"

"I've had guys try and talk me into bondage on the first fuck," Gabriel said slowly. "And one guy locked me in his flat and tried to force me to suck his dick when we'd just met up for a screw and hadn't said anything about playing any games. So I hit him with a lamp and jumped out of the window before he could get his hands on me."

Aled grimaced. "Shit—"

"So yeah, it's never happened, but I'm not naïve," Gabriel said flatly. "Maybe you could be one of the right people. Downstairs was hot as hell, especially the way you just pushed my legs apart like you owned everything between them, but I don't know you well enough to play with you."

"But given time?"

"Maybe."

"Well, I think you gathered downstairs that I'm pretty dominant in the bedroom," Aled said, "but I'm not into that whole constant thing. You know, where you have that dynamic one hundred percent of the time, where the dominant is responsible for literally everything in the submissive's life. I don't like that. Outside of the games, I like—I don't know, vanilla normalcy? You know, bad movie dates, flour fights, weekends away because we don't fancy doing the dishes for a bit. Normal stuff. Like my wife and I would play a pretty brutal rape fantasy, then we'd have a cuddle and a clean-up, and I'd pop out to get fish and chips and we'd eat in our pyjamas on the sofa and watch reruns of old sitcoms."

"You have rape fantasies?" Gabriel asked. He'd gone still and watchful, spoon halfway to his mouth, and Aled mentally patted himself on the back for the guess.

"My wife did. I liked acting them out for her. It does massively turn me on, but it's not a major need of mine."

"So...if I *were* to play games with you, what would you like to do to me?"

Aled paused, then flicked the still-waiting TV off, putting the remote and the bowls on the side before turning over, throwing the duvet back and gently wrapping his fingers around Gabriel's ankles to pull his legs open. He was met with a small, token resistance before Gabriel allowed it, then Aled knelt between them, leaning forward to brace his hands on the headboard either side of Gabriel's face.

If Gabriel lifted his hips, he'd slide right up onto Aled's lap. And his interested cock, which was paying close attention to the proceedings.

Gabriel didn't move, for his part. He stared, watchful and calculating, a tiny hint of a smile at the corner of his mouth, but he didn't move. Aled licked his lips, deciding, then leaned in and kissed him. Gently, but determinedly. He pushed and probed, pulling at Gabriel's lips with his own and nipping them until they darkened, red and swollen, then Aled shifted until he was braced on his forearms, not his hands, and their faces were only inches apart.

And Gabriel's pupils were huge, dark pools.

"I'd use this," Aled murmured, brushing his fingers against Gabriel's hair and tugging slightly. "Control this." He bit at Gabriel's lips again. "You have a beautiful mouth. If I were to play with you, I'd see those lips stretched around my cock as much as possible. Red and swollen and struggling to take it all." He brushed his lips against Gabriel's ear and began to kiss down his neck. "I'd mark this — maybe I'll bite you, maybe I'll put a collar and chain on you. I have a lot of chains and harnesses. Maybe" — he sucked on Gabriel's neck where it disappeared into the borrowed T-shirt — "I would collar you and attach the chain to the headboard, so short you couldn't even sit up. Or to another chain between your ankles, so you'd have to crawl on your hands and knees for me. But you'd be naked, that's for sure." He rubbed his thumb around the hem of the T-shirt, then the waistband of the boxers. "No point in staking a claim by collaring a sub if you're going to have restricted access thanks to their clothes."

Gabriel's answer was to remove Aled's wet fingers from his mouth and guide them down into Aled's boxers, wrap Aled's hand around his own dick and begin to stroke. The slick warmth was a gentle sort of thrill, but it wasn't what Aled wanted, and he casually rearranged their hands so that Gabriel's was on the inside and it was Gabriel's long fingers ghosting up the shaft, squeezing lightly from base to head and rubbing patterns into the pre-cum beginning to bead there.

"I wouldn't have you do much of that," Aled whispered, stooping to kiss Gabriel's nipple through the T-shirt. "I have my own hands. I'd let you get me ready, though. Let you slick me up and sink down onto my cock like you belong on the end of it."

As he spoke, Aled slowly removed his hand — although Gabriel's continued its ministrations — and pulled the hem of the T-shirt up. Progress was stopped by Gabriel's free hand, so Aled tried for the boxers and was permitted. He slid them down to Gabriel's knees and Gabriel performed a circus-worthy contortion and put his feet right up on Aled's shoulders to allow the fabric to be slid over his knee and ankle and be freed.

"I'd *definitely* explore that bendiness," Aled said, tossing the boxers aside and sliding his hands up Gabriel's thighs as his feet drifted back to the mattress. Aled began to knead at his arse, probing his wet fingers and watching Gabriel's face for a hint. When he clenched at the back, but relaxed as Aled stroked past his cunt, Aled smiled. He pushed two fingers inside at once, catching the little hiss with his mouth in a swift, biting kiss.

"I'd not be gentle, if I were playing with you. If you didn't prepare yourself or get my hands and dick nice and wet with that pretty mouth, I'd just fuck you dry."

Gabriel gave a breathy groan and pushed himself down hard on Aled's fingers. Aled stretched them and pulled them out, smoothing his hands down Gabriel's thighs and pulling those pale knees up under his arms before pushing his hands back under Gabriel's arse and lifting ever so slightly.

His intention was clear. And Gabriel's reply was to lift his feet, crossing his ankles over Aled's back, and reach up to grasp the bars of the headboard in both hands. Stretched out. Exposed. In nothing but Aled's T-shirt.

In one swift motion, Aled pulled Gabriel down the pillow and straight onto his cock.

"And sometimes, I'd get you so turned on that you'd slick up my cock yourself and ride it like you were born to do it."

Gabriel groaned and pulled on the headboard, but Aled caught his waist and stopped the motion.

"Not this time."

He dropped his entire weight onto Gabriel's hips, pinning him absolutely in place, and began to thrust. There was no give, no way for Gabriel to move with him, and that was the entire point—Gabriel was left with no choice but to keep his legs open and feel every last inch of Aled's cock. And Aled made sure he felt it, keeping his thrusts long and powerful despite the urge to just bury his teeth in that long, exposed neck and rut. Instead, he bit at whatever skin he could find and dragged his weight along Gabriel's hips and thighs to catch at his pleasure. Aled could feel the mess spreading on his own stomach and Gabriel's aborted shivers and twists as he tried to move, and as Aled felt the pressure becoming too much, Gabriel's hand in his boxers having taken him too far, he seized Gabriel's mouth in a forceful, demanding kiss and came so hard he saw stars.

Then, as the white light in his brain receded, Aled reached down between them and began to stroke.

"Oh God," Gabriel croaked, tightening his thighs around Aled's waist before he began to both grind against Aled's hand and cry. "Fuck, *fuckfuckfuck*—"

"I could do this all night," Aled whispered in his ear, "and if I were to play with you, I might. I could fuck you with a vibrator, then leave it on and tie your legs together so you couldn't push it out. Or I could tie you to a chair in a harness that rubbed a vibrator against you every time you so much as breathed. I could make you come five, ten, fifteen times, until you were so exhausted that you couldn't do anything but move. Then afterwards, when you'd had your five, ten, fifteen turns, I could strip you naked, lock you into a spreader or over a table and keep you there, wide open and ready for it, until I'd used you five, ten, fifteen times myself."

Gabriel made a high, keening cry, seized Aled's wrist and shoved it roughly against his swollen flesh. Aled shifted, his cock still inside Gabriel's pussy, and slowly pierced the only opening left with his thumb.

And Gabriel came. So hard that it hurt Aled's cock, so hard that it expelled his thumb and Gabriel's back arched almost violently. Aled pinned him down, rolling his hips up into the gap between his shuddering thighs, and rode it out, unashamedly staring at the debauched, ruined sight of Gabriel trapped under him and spread around his dick, cum leaking out into the sheets, and shivering like a butterfly caught on a pin through his own orgasm.

When those dark eyes finally cracked open again, Aled leaned down and kissed him gently.

"Then when I was done," he whispered, "I'd plug you, so you'd feel my cum inside you every time you moved."

Gabriel licked his lips and stretched up for another kiss. Aled gave it and made to pull out, only for Gabriel's ankles to tighten on his back and his arse clench around Aled's shaft.

"I think I'd like playing with you," Gabriel croaked. "In time. Later."

"And right now?"

Gabriel cracked a smile and stroked Aled's face sleepily. "Right now, I think I need another shower."

Chapter Twelve

Gabriel stopped at the top of the stairs.

His front door was open.

Immediately, he curled his fist around the key until it stuck out like a knife between his fingers. His phone flicked from his walking home playlist to the first two nines of the emergency number. And he was beyond grateful — suddenly, stupidly, a little insanely — for not having shaved this morning.

"Oi!" he shouted as he inched through the open frame. The flat had been turned over. Drawers open and the contents spilled. The fridge yawning open. Sofa cushions and clothes everywhere. "Get the fuck out of here! I'll call the police!"

"Oh, look, he *lives.*"

Gabriel groaned and dropped the keys onto the side. "Kevin! You dick."

Kevin materialised in his bedroom doorway, arms folded over his barrel chest. He looked thoroughly unamused. There was a grouchy bear in Gabriel's flat, and not the kind of bear he usually liked, either.

"What are you here for anyway?"

"You've not been in touch in a week."

Oh.

Oh.

Gabriel flushed guiltily. Sweat broke out on his palms and not from excitement. "Oh. Shit. Uh. I—lost track of time?"

"How severely I'm going to punish you depends on what you say next."

Yeah, no shit.

Gabriel knew now why the flat looked like a bomb had hit it. Kevin was a good friend, an occasional owner and the closest that Gabriel had to a decent family. And he was the only person in the world whose rules could be applied outside of a sex game—because he was the only person in the world who would drag Gabriel out when he was drowning. He was the only person in the world who cared *all* the time, not just when he was balls-deep in Gabriel's body and biting.

He had rules. Don't walk home alone after the shop had closed for the night. Send postcodes when he was going round to stranger's houses for sex. Let Kevin have his Grindr password so he could see what Gabriel was up to if he was too quiet for too long. Same with the keys to the flat.

Be safe.

But most of all, stay in touch. Even if it was just bitching about the weather or smiley faces, Gabriel was to stay in touch.

And it wasn't even about the sex.

The last time Gabriel hadn't been in touch for more than a week, Kevin had come round to find him surrounded by broken glass in the kitchen, staring at a bottle of vodka and talking to himself. Telling himself that just one drink wouldn't hurt, while his hands were shaking just from the sheer terror of holding it at all. Telling himself he'd be fine, when he hadn't slept in three days and could taste sound.

He'd spent a week locked in Kevin's basement, recovering. Then, when he'd recovered, being punished.

It had kept him sober, when he'd struggled to stick to it. Kevin had held him together when things had threatened to shatter him into pieces. Kevin *cared.* And if Gabriel hadn't been in such a happy sex glow all week, he would have returned the missed calls. Texted once or twice. Even just sent a selfie. *Something.*

So Kevin had been looking for it. The booze. Maybe even drugs, if Gabriel had fallen that far. Something to tell him that Gabriel had fallen off the wagon — something to tell him why there had been nothing on the other end of the phone.

Something he'd not find, because Gabriel had just been stupid instead of struggling.

"Shit," Gabriel said. "I'm sorry."

Kevin raised his eyebrows.

"I've not had a thing, I swear," Gabriel said, raising his hands. "I've been fucking."

"Fucking."

"Yeah. That new guy I told you about. Aled."

"For a week?"

"Well, not every *day...*"

In fact, it had been four days since he'd been to Aled's house. And he'd not seen him since. But that four days —

Aled was kinky. And dominant. And fucked like a machine. And *liked* him. He'd shut away the wine instead of being a dick about it, and they could hold a conversation, and — Aled just *liked* him. Liked his company with his clothes on, not just off. And Gabriel felt the same way. He liked being around Aled. The sex was great, but he could get that anywhere. There was something a little harder to seek out about Aled.

"I really like this guy."

Kevin cocked his head.

"He's funny and he's kind of sweet, but he's the kinky dominant type, too, and —" Gabriel hesitated, then went for it. "I went round his house —"

"You didn't tell me."

" — and — I know, I'm sorry, but listen — and he offered me a glass of wine at the door. And I told him that I can't. I was honest, I even told him about the kissing issue. And he put it all away, did his teeth, mouthwash, the works, then got us both on the lemonade. Just like that." Gabriel snapped his fingers. "Just because — he's nice. He wanted my company. And I spent the night and it was great. I even forgot the wine was there at all. And in the morning, I saw the empty bottle in the recycling bin and he said he'd poured it all away."

Kevin softened.

Sort of.

His stance stayed rock-solid and unyielding, but the scowl on his face disappeared. His dark eyes scanned Gabriel's face, then he slowly nodded.

"Well," he rumbled. "I'm glad you've found someone who's a good fit for you. But that doesn't mean you get to ignore my calls. You know Judith and I get worried."

"I know. And I am sorry."

"Counter."

"Oh, come on!"

Instantly, the warmth drained back out of his voice. "Counter. *Now.*"

Gabriel knew better than to argue. Sighing, he toed off his shoes, then shuffled to the counter in his socks. As Kevin's punishments went, the counter was nothing. *Nothing.* But Gabriel didn't like spanking, and especially not a spanking with Kevin's belt. It always hurt like hell and it didn't even have the common courtesy to get Gabriel off. He'd never understood spanking as a thing and he never would.

But then, he wasn't supposed to enjoy it.

Dropping his trousers, he bent over the sink and spread his knees into the proper position. He heard the clink of Kevin's belt buckle and closed his eyes.

"Usual rules."

Gabriel clenched his jaw. Stupid rules. No movement and no sound. He was allowed to make a noise only if it was to utter his safeword — and that was for *damage.* Because 'it hurts' was not a sufficient excuse when Kevin was punishing him.

A gentle pat. Cold leather on hot skin. A warning.

Then —

The crack was deafening in the silent flat. Fire burst over his bare arse as the leather smashed against him. Gabriel yelped and was immediately struck again for making a noise. He sucked his lips in and bit them, burrowing his head against the bottom of the sink, and tried to relax for the third. God, he hoped it was only ten. *Please only be ten.*

Kevin wore wide belts for heavy jeans and industrial workman's trousers. They *hurt.* If Gabriel had *really* fucked up — like gotten drunk fucked up — Kevin would beat him with the buckle, but thankfully radio silence for a good reason was just the leather. Even so, it was heavy and Kevin had an arm that would make a professional spin bowler jealous. By the seventh blow, Gabriel's legs were shaking. By the ninth, his arse was throbbing in time with his heartbeat. And by the eleventh — he could have sobbed at going past ten — he wanted to cry, piss himself or both.

Then the twelfth faded away and he heard the soft swipe of leather against denim.

Belt loops.

"An extra two for shouting."

Gabriel let out a long, shaking breath.

"What do you say?"

"I'm sorry for not staying in touch," Gabriel whispered.

"And?"

"And it won't happen again."

"If it happens again, it won't just be the counter and a belt."

Gabriel winced. Their sex games were extreme. And Kevin's punishments could be extreme, too.

But also fair. Gabriel knew the rules. He'd accepted them. And when he gingerly straightened up and a hand slid into his hair to massage his scalp, he felt himself relaxing. He stretched into the sensation, then twisted to loop his arms over Kevin's shoulders and cuddle up.

"Status?"

The question was very soft, almost whispered against his ear.

"Green."

Traffic lights. Their safeword system. And despite his arse being on fire, Gabriel *was* green. He had a new regular who was nice and funny and wanted to play. And he had people who worried about him and came looking when he vanished off the face of the earth. Despite the pain, there was a warm softness in his chest, too. He had been in worse places. He had been in places where green didn't exist.

Though he'd have to get better at replying if he wanted to have sex on his back ever again.

"Want to make a curry?" Kevin suggested. "Judith's mum is round and you know how me and Sharon get on."

Gabriel smirked and backed up. "You been kicked out?"

Kevin pulled a face.

"I'll take that as a yes."

"It's not a no. So, let's get a curry going and you can tell me about your new kinky master. He know about me?"

"It's not that far in yet," Gabriel said. "He asked if I was kinky and liked to play, and we had rough sex."

"Least you've had that conversation."

"Yup."

They talked—mainly about Aled—until the curry was simmering on the hob, then retreated to the sofa to find something to watch on the TV. Kevin wasn't like Gabriel's other regulars. He had sex only within his games and those games were very strictly played in his house, preferably the basement. If Gabriel saw Kevin outside the house, then the most sexual he could possibly expect to get was a bit of a kiss, and only then if Gabriel really, *really* needed the affection. Gabriel had a sneaking suspicion that Kevin wasn't capable of getting it up for vanilla sex. God only knew what games had produced his two kids.

So that enormous body sprawled on his sofa was irrelevant to anything energetic. Gabriel handed over the TV remote and went to lie on his front on the floor. He scowled when Kevin chuckled and put his bare feet on Gabriel's back, but otherwise didn't bother to object. Not really much point anyway. At least when the curry was done, Gabriel didn't have to get up to sort it out.

"Come on," Kevin said, once there were two steaming bowls on the coffee table. "Get that down your neck. You look thinner."

"We can't all have Judith's bum."

"You could do with Judith's bum."

"No thanks." Gabriel made a wide gesture around himself. "Hips. These ones are bad enough."

"Shut it," Kevin grunted. "You've got a body people would kill for."

Gabriel knew better than to grumble that he wasn't one of those people. Kevin was confidence all the way down to the bone and had zero ability to put himself in other people's shoes. Great for preventing addiction issues, bloody awful for anything else.

"You know what you need to do, though."

"Eh?"

"If this new bloke is a proper dominant."

Gabriel hummed, prodding the curry.

"Gabriel."

"I know," he said, and sighed. "I'll tell him about you. I just want to enjoy it a bit longer, before I have to dump him."

Because Gabriel didn't do monogamy.

And he didn't trust married men who said they didn't mind.

Chapter Thirteen

Suze pounced the moment that Aled walked out of the building on Friday afternoon.

"Where have you *been*?" she whispered, dragging him by the arm to her car. "You've been ignoring my texts, you wouldn't answer your phone last night —"

Aled grimaced. "Shit, I'm sorry, I —"

"What's going on?"

"Gabriel."

"What, the Grindr guy?"

"Yeah."

"Again?" she asked, then narrowed her eyes. "Sounds like it *is* a fling."

"It's amazing sex," Aled said defensively. "And he came over earlier this week. Stayed the night with me. We had dinner, and —"

"*That* sounds like a date."

Aled cleared his throat. "We had a flour fight and fucked on the kitchen floor," he mumbled, and Suze began to laugh.

"Very nice!"

"And we...talked."

"Boring, get back to the—"

"No, not boring," Aled interrupted quietly. "He's—he's submissive, Suze."

She inhaled sharply.

Suze knew. Of course she knew. Aled had been distraught to learn of his own tastes in sex and had vented all his worries and fears to his best friend from that very first wet dream involving a girl begging him not to hurt her. Suze now teased him for being more wound up about *how* to fuck than who—his bisexuality had never given Aled so much as a pause for thought—but at the time, it had been terrifying. He had never been a violent kid. He'd never been aggressive. Hell, he'd always been considered a bit of a nancy. The other boys at school presumed he was gay for his dislike of spying on the girls' changing rooms with them. The only fights he'd ever gotten in had been with boys talking about girls like they were whores and nothing more—and he'd always lost.

Then along had come the wet dreams about girls crying and offering anything he wanted if he didn't rent them out to his friends to fuck for him, about beating boys until they could barely move, then fucking them for daring to say no to him—

He'd been terrified. And Suze, his best friend from before he could remember, had been there to hold him through the panic and figure out, right beside him, what the hell was going on. So of course she knew. And she knew why that discovery was not in the least bit boring.

"I—did a couple of things. Nothing serious, just...you know, I told him to be good, I pushed him up against this wall to fuck him the first time we met. The other night, I had him up against the fridge and he started talking. And he was saying...you know, fairly submissive things."

"Like?"

Aled glanced around the parking area, but there was nobody around. "Harder. Deeper. Use him. That sort of thing."

"*Use* him?"

"Yeah," Aled said significantly. "So, after, we talked. And he admitted he plays games sometimes and maybe if we keep on the way we are and he comes to trust me a bit more, he'd play with me."

Suze's face split into a huge grin. "Oh my God, you jammy bastard!"

Aled laughed.

"Seriously! The *first* guy you try after — well, after — and he's absolutely gorgeous and likes to bend over and grab his ankles on command!"

Aled's face exploded in heat. "Suze, shut up!"

She just laughed at him some more and Aled groaned.

"God, why do I tell you anything?"

"Because I'm amazing," she said. "Did he say what kind of games?"

"No, but he...hinted at something like rape fantasies. And we talked about mine. And I fucked him again, telling him what I'd do to him, things like collar him and chain him up and he really liked that."

"Oh my God," she repeated, beaming. "So this is a developing thing, then? So much for your one-night stand."

Aled shrugged, grinning stupidly at his shoes. "I guess so."

"Admit it," Suze said, "this sounds a lot like moving on."

Aled paused. The words were stark and jarring, and he hesitated.

"I—" *Am I? Really?* "I'm not in love with him, Suze."

"You don't have to fall in love again to be moving on."

"Except for the part where I still love Melissa."

"Would you give up this for her?"

Aled frowned. "Yes. I would. To have—to have my *wife* back, to get back to the life we're supposed to be having *together*. I like Gabriel, Suze, but he's just fun. It's fun. It's a distraction. It's not a relationship. I don't love him."

"But you could," Suze said quietly.

Aled swallowed and shook his head. "No, I couldn't."

"Aled, I'm your best friend. I know what you're like when you're infatuated and *this* is it. You met up with this guy for a one-night stand to get yourself back in the game and now you're telling me it's been a few times and you've talked about playing games together? You might not love him, but he's not exactly just a pretty arse, is he?"

Aled ground his teeth. "Don't talk about him like that."

Suze raised her eyebrows.

"Admit it," she said. "You're attracted to him. For more than his performance against fences and fridges."

Aled groaned. "Fine. Maybe I do. Maybe he's fun and he's easy-going and he takes my mind off the fucking train wreck that I've been left with—is that a crime?"

"Of course it's not," Suze said flatly, "but you can't bury your head in the sand and pretend it's just about getting off, either. It's not healthy."

"Fuck healthy," Aled said bitterly.

"I want you to move on," Suze snapped. "Melissa isn't coming back. It's nice to see you finally figuring out there's other people out there who can make you feel good. Just—this is how you lose that kind of thing."

"Lose him? What, because I love my wife? Suze, he's slept with half of Yorkshire. This is just sex to him, too. It's not a relationship."

"If it's more than a couple of times, it's some kind of relationship," Suze said tartly, getting her car keys out of her handbag. "Just don't ruin things for yourself by pretending things aren't changing, Aled. I don't want to see you do that to yourself."

"I'm not—!"

But he never got the last word with Suze. She unlocked her car and slammed the door on him, leaving Aled to seethe and simmer and—

Admit, perhaps, that she might have a point. It wasn't just sex. Not purely, not a hundred per cent. But it wasn't—couldn't be, *wasn't*—anything more. Not if he wanted to fix things with Melissa and he did. He always would.

Sighing, Aled rummaged for his own keys and headed over to his car. Even that reminded him of Melissa. It had been a present from her father, with a nudge and a wink and a joke about it being too difficult to get baby seats in and out of the three-door Corsa they'd had before. As he peeled out into the rush-hour traffic, Aled wondered if he ought not to just sell it and buy something else. Some nice flash sports car. Something with a wide back seat for Gabriel to spread his legs on.

He shook himself. Jesus, if that didn't sound like a mid-life crisis. He wasn't even *old* enough for a mid-life crisis.

He pulled up at the gym but then sat in the car with the engine running, staring at his phone instead. He didn't want to go in, but he didn't want to go home, either. The sight of the empty bed, where he'd taken Gabriel like a sex slave, framed by his wedding photograph and Melissa's graduation headshot on the side tables, would hurt. It would hurt and Aled didn't know whether he wanted to strip the bed again and erase all and any evidence of Gabriel's presence there, or — or remove the pictures.

Then he felt sick at the idea of taking down the last of his wife's pictures because he'd fucked a self-proclaimed slut in their bed.

What was he supposed to do?

Gabriel made him feel good. Burying his cock in that beautiful body, kissing the sweat from his shoulders and fisting his hands in that ink-dark hair — it all made Aled feel good again. Good like he hadn't for a year, good like he hadn't for maybe more than that. But it was a betrayal. Melissa didn't know about Gabriel — how could she? — and they had always been honest when either of them had played away. He would have told her. And he would have slept with Gabriel once, and only once, and that would have been that. Instead, he'd used Gabriel's body like a sheath for his dick several times, covered their kitchen and sheets in the evidence of it, without a second thought about the fact that he was married, still married, and what was he supposed to do, just brush it off as not counting because they were separated?

If he seriously wanted to get Melissa back, then why in the hell was he playing around with Gabriel? Why was he considering playing *games* with Gabriel?

He ought to say no.

He ought to stop all of this.

But –

But he hadn't felt so good in so long. It was like a drug. Gabriel was like snorting coke – he could bring Aled back to life with one smile, one touch, one kiss. Coming in his hands was like dying and being reborn as a whole new person. And watching Gabriel get off was like looking into the face of God. Unbelievably, unfathomably magnificent.

He squeezed the phone until he heard the case creak.

He *should* walk. But he *wanted* to stay.

And how long since Aled had just let go and let himself do whatever he wanted? He'd gone through all that prodding and poking at the hospital because of what Melissa wanted. He'd even met up with Gabriel in the first place because it was what Tom and Suze wanted. And right now, *he* wanted. *He* wanted to talk boundaries and games. *He* wanted to have sex, maybe meaningless and maybe not. *He* wanted to skip swimming and go to Belle Isle and have an entirely different kind of workout.

Why the fuck not?

Me: You free? Got designs on your dick. Then maybe we can talk? x

There was no immediate reply, but he tossed the phone aside and rolled the car back out of the gym car park. He'd go home, get some dinner and a shower and by then Gabriel would have surfaced from wherever he was — or whoever was in him — and texted back. Aled didn't even care if it was a case of sloppy seconds at this point. He just wanted to have a bit of bloody *fun*.

But all notion of fun evaporated out of his system when he got home and saw the corner of brown envelope sticking out of the letterbox.

"Fuck," he whispered.

Wildly hoping he'd missed a payment to the TV licensing people, he opened the front door as gingerly as if the package could be a bomb. But it was worse.

It was crumpled and the envelope a little torn, as if it had been roughly forced through the letterbox, and when Aled turned it over, the return address was to a solicitor's office in Huddersfield.

The same solicitor on the last packet.

Melissa's.

Aled closed his eyes, suddenly feeling sick. How had they gotten here? He'd loved Melissa ever since he was fourteen, had vowed to be with her forever, had married her with every intention of adhering to 'until death do us part'. And now he was standing in his hall, holding the second pack of divorce paperwork she'd tried to give him and planning a conversation with a man he met on Grindr about whether or not Aled would be allowed to chain him up in the basement and use him like a sex slave on Saturday nights.

God, how had it fucking come to this?

His phone buzzed in his pocket and Aled stormed into the kitchen, shoving the envelope in the back of a drawer. He couldn't deal with that. Not now. He was — he was going to take Gabriel out to dinner and find out his dealbreakers and persuade him that Aled wasn't dangerous to play with.

Not this. Not this, not a divorce, not losing her, not this.

Aled breathed, his fingers trembling, and shook his head. *Fuck.* It was too late. The plan was careering away from him. He couldn't do this. Not now, not today. *Fuck. Fuck!*

He twisted and slammed his fist into the plaster by the doorframe. The plaster crumbled and the pain that lanced up his forearm cleared his thoughts. He was too upset for this. His head was in bits and he wouldn't really hear whatever Gabriel told him. He'd either end up hurting Gabriel or hurting himself by mistaking resistance for the sake of the game as resistance for the sake of consent.

"Fuck," he whispered and fumbled for his phone. The buzz had been a text from Gabriel and Aled swallowed, dialling.

"Hey! So I'm—"

"I'm sorry," Aled interrupted. "It's been a bloody shitty day and I know what I just said, but I'm in completely the wrong place to do it right now."

Gabriel made a quiet noise. "Are you okay?"

"Just—shit day."

"Well, you always say I make you feel good. Come over anyway and we'll forgo the talk and I'll just make you feel good."

Aled laughed quietly. "I appreciate the offer, but right now—"

"Not *right* now. You're obviously too wound up. Tell you what. Pub, dinner, a couple of rounds of pool and whoever loses gives the winner a blowjob in your car after. Deal?"

Aled smiled sadly at the crumbled plaster, pushing at it hypnotically with his finger. His knuckles were

The Divorce

scraped and bruised and he'd need to shower to get the dust off and put some antiseptic cream over the damage. It would be really late by the time he got there.

"I won't be at yours until at least half-seven."

"That's fine. You might have relaxed by then anyway and I can blow you before we leave."

"You won't have lost by then."

"I suck at pool. Trust me, *you* win in this arrangement."

"I'm shit as well."

"Well, fuck. Are you any good at darts?"

"Not unless you want me to Hawkeye some poor bastard fifty feet from the dartboard."

"What?"

"Okay," Aled said, rallying himself, "I need to sit you down and give you a proper course in geekery."

"Oh no you don't—"

"Oh yes I do. And thanks," Aled interrupted when Gabriel spluttered. "Just...for being nice about things and not asking."

"Never ask, just commiserate," Gabriel said cheerily. "Come and get me and your blowjob for half-seven and we'll go down and you can kick my arse at pool and I can blow you a second time for, say, ten?"

"Ten sounds good. See you soon."

As Aled hung up, he shook himself, as though shaking off rain, and squared his shoulders. Hot shower. First aid kit on his hand. Then, apparently, blowjob.

He didn't have to think about the post until the morning anyway.

* * * *

Dinner was a good idea.

Pool was not.

By the time the table was free, Aled had forgotten all about the divorce paperwork. And by the time they had finished the first frame, he'd forgotten that he'd been having a bad day at all. Mostly because Gabriel was wearing very tight jeans and pool involved a lot of bending over the table.

Especially as Gabriel refused to use a rest.

He was hot as the surface of the sun and Aled wasn't ashamed to stare along with a fair few women in the pub. Gabriel was packing, the jeans showing off a decent bulge in his crotch, and it made them cling even more to his backside. The long T-shirt hid the curve of his hips but was tight across his upper chest and shoulders. He was wearing something to flatten his tits and every time he bent over the table to take a shot, Aled wanted to rip his jeans down and fuck him bloody—but he couldn't. And a tiny part of his brain absolutely hated Gabriel at that moment, for the trick Aled knew he'd pulled. Innocent, friendly game of pool to lift Aled's spirits, his shapely arse.

Although…it *was* lifting said spirits.

"I know what you're up to," he said as Gabriel set up the second game.

"What?"

"Trying to distract me."

"Nothing to do with distraction."

Aled snorted and Gabriel laughed.

"It's not!" he said and grinned. Aled regarded him warily. "I told you, I suck at pool anyway, I couldn't win unless you totally lost your shit and fucked me on the table." A couple of nearby girls stared. "I'm not trying to distract you."

Aled groaned. "So you're trying to get laid."

"Always."

"Well, it's working. Stop it," Aled groused, but in truth, he quite liked it. Nothing like someone actively trying to get in his jeans to rally his opinion of himself. "I have a question."

"Shoot."

"Have you always been so…sexual, or it is from the hormones?"

"Who says I take hormones?"

"Your three-day-old semi-beard says you take hormones."

Gabriel smirked. "Maybe I'm just naturally fuzzy."

"Nobody without a liberal amount of testosterone has arms that fluffy." Gabriel's arm hair — and leg hair, actually — was still a source of complete shock to Aled. Someone with limbs that hairy ought, by rights, to be a certified werewolf. And yet his back and chest were almost completely hairless, and his face took a couple of days to get going.

"Could be intersex."

"Are you?"

"Not that I know of," Gabriel admitted, taking a shot and missing spectacularly.

"So you take hormones."

"Yep."

"So…?"

"So, I've always been like this," Gabriel said, "but in the week after a shot, I'm definitely hornier. Six of one, half a dozen of the other."

"How often do you have a shot?"

"Every four weeks."

"So once a month, I'm almost guaranteed to get laid if I come round?"

"Definitely guaranteed."

Aled grinned and Gabriel narrowed his eyes.

"Don't make the monthly visitor joke," he warned and Aled held up his hands.

"Wouldn't dream of it."

Gabriel rolled his eyes as he narrowly missed fouling off the black and said, "Can I ask a question?"

"Seems fair."

"Why the lack of questions?"

Aled blinked. "Uh—"

"That's the first time you've mentioned it."

"Well…"

"Don't get me wrong, constantly having to be a teacher when it comes to this stuff is exhausting and kind of sucks sometimes, but honestly, sometimes someone asking no questions whatsoever is a bigger red flag than getting grilled."

"What do you mean?"

"It becomes an elephant in the room. I mean, seriously, even people who know other people like me want to talk about it."

Aled squirmed uncomfortably. "I—"

"It just seems like you're avoiding the subject. Which can feel just as shit as someone slagging you off for it, to be honest."

Aled winced. "I don't mean that—"

"I know you don't. I'm just saying."

"I guess I don't ask a lot of questions because…well, it's not my business," Aled said awkwardly.

"Not your business doesn't stop anyone talking about something ever."

"True." Aled sank the ball, waved Gabriel to set up again and pondered. "I suppose because it doesn't change anything about me, I didn't feel like I ought to ask."

"How do you mean?"

"Well, you said about that guy the other day that he figured if he, uh, you know, you didn't make him not straight."

"Right—"

"I don't change no matter what you are," Aled said baldly. "I've had both. I'll always like both. So I guess...I don't know, it's visually odd but there's nothing I've not seen before, maybe?"

"So you have questions, you just thought it would be rude to ask."

"Well, yeah. You always get told don't ask, it's none of your business, you know?" Aled said. "Almost like it's rude to be curious these days."

Gabriel laughed. "Oh, I have no problem with curiosity."

"You don't talk about it, though."

"I don't much like to," Gabriel admitted as he slotted the balls into place, "but you learn to pick apart curiosity from cuntishness. And there's *always* curiosity. Everyone on earth wants to comment on it when they find out, so when you find someone who doesn't, it can be cuntishness all on its own."

"Cuntishness," Aled said flatly, "is not a word."

"And I do not care, O Graduate of Pendanticity."

"Nor is that."

Gabriel pulled a face and punished Aled by taking the break in the most bent-over, long-winded, arse-wiggling way he could possibly manage. The conversation was thoroughly derailed and Aled swallowed against a dry throat, his jeans uncomfortably tight where they'd fit fine a moment ago.

"That's on purpose," he croaked.

"Mm," Gabriel said, breaking — poorly — and smirking at Aled's situation. He wandered around the table, a little too slow and his eyes a little too dark, and said, "You've won two games and there's only one remaining. If you want to forfeit this one, you still win."

"Loser blows winner."

"Yep. Want to get to that part?"

Aled swallowed. "Or...or a bit more. I could explore. Ask some questions."

"Sounds good. Your place or mine?"

"Yours. It's closer. No way can I drive back to Wakefield like this," Aled said hoarsely and Gabriel laughed, openly palming him in the middle of the pub and causing the little spare blood that Aled had to flood his face and burn it hot.

"Tell you what," Gabriel whispered, very close and very quiet. "Find us a layby and I'll let you ask all the questions you want."

Not taking his eyes off Gabriel, Aled casually reached out, took hold of the black and placed it firmly in the nearest pocket.

"I lose," he said. "Now get the fuck in my car."

Chapter Fourteen

"So what do you call this?" Aled asked.

Gabriel unglued his eyes and blinked sleepily at the ceiling. Were those even words? God, his brain was fried.

"W't?"

"This." A finger gently pierced him. Some remaining cum slid free and Gabriel clenched to hold it in.

"S'my cunt, dipshit."

Aled chuckled. "Then?"

The cumstained finger stroked his aching, exhausted cock, and Gabriel whimpered.

"Sorry. Tender?"

"Suck me again and find out."

"Suck your what?"

"My cock," Gabriel mumbled. "You need an anatomy lesson?"

"Practice makes perfect," Aled quipped, but — to Gabriel's annoyance — he didn't get his hand up in where his tongue and cock had already visited. Instead, he wiped his fingers off on the sheet and pushed himself up out of the bed.

"Hey!"

"I need to piss."

Gabriel grumbled. He kicked the sheets off and stretched. Everything ached. Aled had eaten him out like he was the steak platter on a *Man Vs Food* challenge, then—after he'd already gotten Gabriel off twice and reduced him to mindless gibbering—had rammed his cock in there and hammered him only three or four times before coming and leaving what felt like a flood behind. Gabriel was fairly sure he was leaking, with or without the casual fingering.

He had to wear those jeans again.

And they had to have that talk, he decided. It was hot—but it would have been a thousand times hotter if Aled had tied his heads to the headboard and shoved a sock in his mouth when he'd fucked him. A clean sock. Gabriel didn't want to get *too* nasty, but a sock all the same.

He blinked.

His tit was hot.

Gabriel yawned and realised that he must have dozed off. The sheets were back. There was someone snoring in his ear. The scratchy sensation of dried cum on his skin. And his left nipple was *incredibly* hot.

Gabriel frowned as his brain started to come online. Why the hell would—

The body at his back shifted with a low mumble and the hand that had glued itself to his naked breast contracted lightly.

Oh.

He sighed and dislodged the hand. Typical. Gay or bisexual, hands *always* ended up on his tits when he slept shirtless with someone. And ninety per cent of the time, they migrated there even if he had a shirt on. He yawned again and freed himself. Dried cum was trying to glue his labia together and it wasn't a great feeling. *Shower*.

He took his time, washing away all the evidence, then scrubbing himself down with an exfoliating sponge. Aled had been biting again. His neck was a rainbow of bruises and there was a perfect outline of some decent dentistry on his inner thigh. He hadn't even noticed the tit-chewing, but that same left nipple was swollen and sore. He slapped some antiseptic cream and a plaster on it, then went hunting in the fridge.

It was half past five in the morning. The sky was still black as tar and it had been snowing lightly overnight. Gabriel checked the calendar and punched the air when he realised he didn't have to go to work. And it being a Saturday, surely Aled didn't either? Grinning, he added more eggs to the mix and went rummaging for the big pan.

"What are you doing?"

He jumped at the deep, raspy question. Aled had materialised in the bedroom doorway. His hair was sticking up and he was completely naked. And wanking idly, his half-hard cock getting fuller by the second in his hand.

"Not you?"

"Wrong answer," Aled growled and everything in Gabriel's body went south. He stood frozen as Aled crossed the room, and whimpered when a hand gripped the back of his neck and pressed down. *Counter*, his mind whispered, but there was no belt. He shuddered as knees pressed between his own and parted them and a long shaft slid neatly up against him.

Then inside.

He whined as he was filled. Slow. Relentless. It was an unyielding pressure that climbed all the way up inside him until he felt impaled. Imprisoned. Weight pressed down on his back and head, pinning him to the kitchen counter.

Trapped.

And it felt so fucking *good.*

He curled his hands into fists on the counter as he was massaged from the inside by that insatiable dick. The thrusts were nothing more than soft rolls of the hips pressing up against his own. The head scraped back, then pushed in like it was the last stroke every time, and when he clenched — for more, to have it harder, to be *fucked* instead of idly screwed — the hand on the back of his neck tightened in warning.

But Gabriel didn't like to just relax and let sex happen. It was boring. It was always too gentle. The mental sensation was nice — being used, being a service — but there was no physical burn, no adrenaline, no kick. He wanted to wriggle. He wanted to be ploughed. He wanted to feel it all the way up to his teeth.

But every time he tried, Aled just bore down. He wouldn't fuck. He would crush, smother, flatten, even smack — a sharp reprimand on the wrist when Gabriel tried to reach back and grab Aled's hair — but he wouldn't *fuck.*

He came suddenly. The flood of wet heat was almost disappointing. He froze inside Gabriel for the longest moment, then his lips brushed his ear.

"Don't move."

"Wha—"

The withdrawal was sharp and left Gabriel empty and cold. A trickle of cum leaked down the back of his leg — but he obeyed. He stayed perfectly still. Heard footsteps padding into the bedroom. Heard a drawer bang. The footsteps coming back.

"Jesus," he whined when a tongue licked a heavy stripe from his knee to his arse, cleaning away the spilled cum. Then he lost the power of words altogether when a familiar coolness pressed up against him.

"Found your toys."

He whined as the dildo sank into him. It was *wide.* And usually one for punishment. It was the one Kevin would lock into his arse when he'd misbehaved. It was the one that made it hard to walk. Flickers of pain radiated out into his hips as it was pushed deeper, deeper, *deeper* —

"There."

He gasped when it bottomed out, throbbing all around it. And Aled had pushed it all the way in and Gabriel's own lips kissed the base of it and he took a gulping, hitching breath when Aled's tongue traced the back of it, cleaning him.

"Thought you were making breakfast?"

"F-fuck."

"Figured that could keep you busy until I've recharged."

Very carefully, Gabriel pushed himself upright. The rod buried inside him rubbed in all the right — wrong — places, and his knees shook. Aled laughed and his hands were warm and oddly tame at Gabriel's waist.

"You can finish breakfast," Gabriel whispered, seizing Aled's hair in a fist and spitting the words at his mouth from inches away. "I'm going to lie down."

Aled took a step forward. It shoved Gabriel up against the counter once more and fingers pinched his arse. He twitched, then yelped as his own muscles briefly fucked him on that cock.

"Finish breakfast with that driving you crazy," Aled whispered against his mouth, "and I will fuck you so hard it hurts after. Any way you want."

Gabriel seized it.

"Even if I tell you to tie me to the bed and fuck me so hard the bed breaks?"

There was a long pause.

"You wanted that talk," Gabriel whispered. "So do I."

Aled's throat bobbed in his neck. Gabriel leaned in and licked it.

"Fuck me until I lose my mind," he whispered. "Then we can talk until Monday morning if that's what you want."

Aled kissed him.

Cupped his face and kissed him. Open. Sweet. Almost loving. Gabriel's knees shivered again and it was nothing to do with the toy buried to the base in his pussy. There was something else lingering around the edges of the way Aled touched him and Gabriel wanted to find it.

"It's an iron-framed bed," Aled whispered against his mouth.

Gabriel smiled. "Well, if you're not going to put the effort in—"

Teeth. His lip. He whined and a tongue licked the protest away.

Then Aled patted his bum and backed up.

"Deal. You finish breakfast—then I'll finish you."

Chapter Fifteen

Aled yielded to delivering on the fuck before the talk.

He didn't tie Gabriel up, but he held his hips in both hands and fucked into him with the hardest rhythm he could manage. It had been a while since he'd done a piston-fuck — Melissa hadn't been too much of a fan — and by the time Gabriel was begging to come, Aled's legs were asking why the hell he thought this marathon was a good idea without so much as a warm-up stretch.

But it was worth it, for the blissed-out look on Gabriel's face and the discovery that he was cuddly as all hell after a brutal drilling.

Even if he did accuse Aled of making him look chaste.

"I'm feeling good," was Aled's only explanation.

"Mm. Wouldn't be anything to do with you sweet-talking me into kinky games, would it?"

Aled shrugged, pushing himself up to watch as Gabriel abandoned the bed and gathered clothes. "Partly. Also partly that...I don't know, I've missed sleeping with someone in the literal sense, too. I guess I've been lonely."

"So is the octopus routine going to wear off, or —"

"Yeah, no. No, it won't."

"Christ, I'll need the summer duvet…"

Aled laughed and threw back the sheet to follow Gabriel into the bathroom. The shower was too small to take together, but they swapped with soft kisses, then wandered out to the sofa together in matching towels.

"So, are you still willing to try out some scenes with me?"

Gabriel put his damp feet up on the coffee table and switched the TV on, turning the volume down low. "Maybe. Depending on what we talk about."

Aled waited for him to find a show before reaching out a hand and turning it over, beckoning with his fingers. Gabriel blinked, then slipped his hand into Aled's and squeezed.

"Have you done BDSM before?"

"Yes."

"I don't mean have you played around with handcuffs, I mean —"

"I have a regular guy who chains me in his basement and beats me if I make a noise while he's fucking me," Gabriel deadpanned. "Yes, I've done the real deal. What I've not done is be the…exclusive guy."

"What do you mean?"

"Are you only screwing me?"

"Yeah."

"So I'm the only one you're interested in playing games with right now?"

"Yeah — ah. I see."

"Mm."

"Okay," Aled said and tightened his grip on Gabriel's hand again. "I want you. That other people want you?

That they have you? Don't care. I'm not after exclusive."

Gabriel cocked his head. "Other guys climb all the way up inside me and fuck me senseless. Regularly. On Wednesday, I had make-up sex with one of my other regulars and I rode his face like a saddle. Next week I'm meeting up with someone I know off Tinder and that always leads to hotel room sex. Sometimes when you find me loose and ready, it's because there's been another dick there within the hour."

Aled laughed. He knew that talk. He'd had that talk before. Not so crudely — nor quite so sex-focused — but it was the same one Melissa had given him when he'd asked her to marry him. That it would never be just him. That he was *a* one, but never *the* one.

"Gabe."

" —riel."

"Sorry. Gabriel. I don't care."

The wary side-eye eased.

"I'm not asking for exclusive. But I like you and I like sleeping with you and I'd like to do more of it."

Gabriel relaxed back into the cushions and nodded.

"Likewise," he said awkwardly. "So — what kind of sleeping?"

"Games?"

"Sex, games, whatever you want to call it."

Aled blew up into his hair. "So...can I put a disclaimer on the front of all of this?"

"Sure."

"If the answer is no, then it's no and that's fine."

"Sorry, what?"

"I know what I like," Aled said flatly. "I think you know what you like. I just want to find the stuff that overlaps and we can do together. I'm not interested in experimenting or justifying anything, so if there's something that either of us don't want to do, we don't do it. End of story."

A faint smile crept onto Gabriel's otherwise impassive face.

"I don't need an explanation," Aled said. "I mean, I'd *like* one, so I can avoid any triggers you might have, so I can spot any patterns in what would affect you badly, but I don't need one. All you need to say is no. And I'd expect the same in return. There's certain things I can't do, won't do, and one or two of them I'm not ready to explain to you yet. But I'll say no if you ask for them and I expect you to respect that."

Gabriel's grip tightened a little and Aled rubbed his thumb over the knuckles.

"You said you have some intense fantasies."

Gabriel's jaw tightened. "You said you have rape fantasies."

"Yes," Aled said flatly.

"You want to rape me?"

"No," Aled said instantly and shook the caught hand. The question jarred, his own insecurities surging forward, but he tamped them down. It was — much as he hated it — a sensible challenge. Gabriel didn't know him, really. Gabriel didn't know his expectations, his experience. Despite his loathing of the word, and its use anywhere near him, Aled almost…appreciated Gabriel's near-hostility. This wasn't a man about to be coerced. "Absolutely not. And if I did, we wouldn't be having this discussion."

The smile widened.

"I get it. You're wary. I'm effectively a stranger still and you're taking a leap of faith to play any kind of game with me," Aled said quietly. "And we'll start off slow. I'm not going to jump straight from morning sex to kidnapping you and keeping you in a cage for a week."

Gabriel took his hand back and folded his arms. He hunched his shoulders, leaning forward towards the TV, and exhaled. A barrier had gone up and Aled watched it carefully.

"So, start off slow," Gabriel said. "But I need to know this first. Why do you do it? What gets you off?"

Aled licked his lips. "Power," he said finally. "I like to dominate. My partner being at my mercy — that gets me off. Could be physically — could tie you up, beat you, slap you around — or mentally. Humiliate you. Call you a whore, make you crawl on the floor, film you. I get off on subjugating you, but…not all the time."

"What does that mean?"

"Sometimes I'll want you to be submissive, to give in. To drop your eyes and call me sir, just be a submissive slave and do as you're told," Aled said. "And sometimes, I'll want you to fight me. To fight back, to refuse to do it, to make me force you to do it. Sometimes I want to have to *take* control, not have it handed to me."

Gabriel swallowed. "All the time?"

Aled laughed. "Oh God, no."

Gabriel's shoulders relaxed. It was like a rubber band had snapped and Aled realised what had been bothering him.

"I *really* don't like that extending outside of the scenes," he said. "That subjugation thing, it's sexual. That's all. I can't stand that outside of sex. I want — the rest of the time, I want you to be *you*. I want you to backchat me. I want to have — have stupid movie dates with you and laugh at people ice-skating and you to call me a berk when I'm being one. All that dominance, all that aggression…it's just about sex for me. I don't like it anywhere else. I'm not like that any other time. It freaks me the fuck out when it's not about sex."

Gabriel was relaxing and he nodded slowly.

"So when it comes to sex, you might want to fuck my mouth until I choke and beat me when I refuse. Or—or kidnap me off the streets and fuck me in the back of your car before tossing me out again. Or come home and have your cock sucked at the door by your pretty pet in a collar—"

Aled shifted uncomfortably, adjusting himself, and Gabriel coughed a brief laugh.

"All of the above," Aled admitted.

"But then after, it's all…game over, let's have a Chinese and watch *EastEnders*."

"I am never watching *EastEnders* in my life, but yeah, that's the gist of it."

Gabriel nodded and slowly slid his fingers back into Aled's. "Okay. I'm okay with that."

"Yeah?"

"Yeah. Sort of."

Aled frowned. "Sort of?"

"I told you, I'm not exclusive. There're other guys. There'll always be other guys. And—"

"And, that's fine," Aled interrupted, squeezing his fingers. "I'm not asking you to be. And if you don't want me including mention of it—"

"You can mention it all you like," Gabriel said. "I like dirty talk. I'm hardly going to safeword you if you bend me over the footboard and call me a whore. But you don't get to punish me for it. You can't demand of me that I give up other guys."

Aled played with his fingers. "If I scened you and said I'd seen you in town with some other guy and I was going to fuck you until you remembered who you belonged to, would that be okay?"

"Fuck me until I remember? Yes."

"So if I said I'd seen you with some other guy and I was going to punis—"

"No."

Aled nodded. "All right. No problem."

"Yeah?"

"Yeah, no problem. Like I said, I'm not asking for you to be exclusive. And I'll say things in scenes all the time that I don't mean, or that aren't problems. I'll certainly call you a whore if you're okay with me saying it, but it doesn't mean I believe it."

"You can't punish me for it. That's all."

"Fine," Aled said. "So you like dirty talk?"

"Mhmm."

"Could I use toys on you? Plugs, dildos, vibrators, that kind of thing?"

Gabriel looked pointedly towards the kitchenette, where the used dildo was soaking in the sink.

"Er...other toys?" Aled amended, feeling the heat rush to his face. "Sorry, stupid question."

Gabriel smirked but shrugged. "I'm not a fan of nipple clamps. I don't mind you playing with my tits a bit with your fingers and teeth, but I don't like toys there. Or harnesses. It feels wrong. Other toys are okay. You know, the standard stuff. Just let me see them before you use them and I'll safeword anything too weird."

"And your other guys? Can I threaten you with them?"

Gabriel paused. "You can threaten. But you can't make me."

"What do you mean?"

"If I want to fuck someone, I fuck them. You don't get to tell me who to fuck. Ever. But if—if we previously agreed it, like literally before we start the scene previous, we're having a threesome or whatever, then in that scene you could tell me you were…I don't know, renting me out to this guy, or he'd asked to fuck me too and I have no choice, fine—but not spontaneously."

"But I could say it in theory? Like…if you don't behave, I'll take you down to the club and let the bouncers fuck your arse until it's bleeding?"

"Yeah. You just couldn't actually do that."

Aled nodded. "Okay. Bondage?"

"Fine."

"Thank God for that," he said and Gabriel laughed. "Blindfolds?"

"Fine."

"Gags?"

"Um, sort of? Not with bondage at first. Later on, yeah, but I need that trust first."

"I wouldn't use any until I'd learned to read you better anyway," Aled assured him. "And we'd rig up something for safewording if you couldn't speak." Gabriel nodded. "What about filming it?"

"Not yet."

"Other people watching?"

"Not yet."

"In public?"

Gabriel smirked. "Well, we already did—"

Aled laughed. "That was just sex, though."

"Could have been more. You *did* slam me against a wall and tell me to be good."

"True."

"Don't get me arrested. That's all."

"No problem, I'd be nicked too, and no thanks." Aled rubbed his thumb over Gabriel's knuckles, eyeing his face and running scenarios through his head, wondering. "What about pain?"

"Not extreme stuff."

"Like?"

"Fucking cutting bits off and shit, that's what!"

Aled grinned. "I'm not *that* kinky. Relax. Could I – I don't know – put a cigarette out on you?"

"No, no burns. But you can hit me, that sort of thing. It doesn't really get me off on its own, but the atmosphere can."

"So limited point for you?"

"Yeah."

Aled nodded. "What's your strict nos?"

"If it involves shit or piss, it doesn't involve me."

"Fair enough."

"And you can't – God, this is going to sound weird…"

"Hey, no judging."

"You can't – I don't know how to explain it, but you can't call me trans."

"Ever?"

"When we're playing," Gabriel clarified. "Like you can't – I don't know, you can't call me a tranny whore, or say I'm trans so I'm this or that – "

Aled frowned.

"But you *can*, like, use the front. You can say I have a cunt, you can threaten to fuck it, or whatever, but you can't say, like, 'this is what girls are for' or 'you want to be a man, I'll fuck you like one', that kind of thing."

"So I can be perfectly aware and show I'm aware that you have, er, the plumbing, but not comment on it beyond its existence?"

"Yeah."

"Is that a—"

"It's a huge trigger," Gabriel mumbled, glancing down, and Aled brought his hand up to kiss the knuckles.

"Hey," he said softly. "No triggers, all right? Told you. A no is all I need to hear."

"Then no."

"Done," Aled said firmly and Gabriel offered him a small smile. "So no shit or piss, your status is to be kept out of things—anything else?"

"No drowning. And no actual torture—I mean, you know, threaten me with it, fine, but I'm really not into having my fingernails ripped off or being sleep-deprived for days."

"Christ! Well, that's one of my nos as well, so we're good there."

Gabriel offered a smile, a little more relaxed than before, and said, "What are yours? And don't give me any of that 'oh, I'm the dominant' shit. You still must have some."

"I do. And given *what* I fantasise about doing, and what gets me off, the biggest one is that you *have* to use your safewords. I don't care when or why or how, but you've got to use them, and I have to trust you to do it. So test me. Push me. Chuck them at me when I'm obviously enjoying myself and see what I do. I need to know you'll use them because…look, I have issues with this. I do. I enjoy it when I'm doing it, then later, it'll start up in the back of my head—what kind of sick fuck gets off pretending that he's raping his partner, what kind of bastard wants his partner to be crying and begging him to stop before he comes on their face?"

"Aled—"

"And if I can't trust that you *will* use them, that'll latch on to it and say you *wanted* to, but you were afraid to. And that would—fuck, if I ever found out I *had* raped someone, it'd destroy me. I might be a dominant, I might have fantasies, but I'm not an abuser. I'm not a fucking rapist."

Gabriel was squeezing his hand so hard that it hurt and Aled had to take a shaky breath to calm himself.

"I will," Gabriel said softly. "Promise. I'll want to put you through the wringer anyway, you know. If you're ever going to carry on when I've used a safeword, then I need to know so I can bail on this like…yesterday."

Aled summoned up a smile and blew out a breath. "I also—don't say my name. In scenes. It feels too…personal, too much like it's really me, really abusing someone, and it gets to me. So if we're playing anything remotely violent or abusive, don't."

"Just the violent, abusive ones?"

"Yes. The already-trained submissive ones, you'll call me what I tell you to call me, usually sir. But if it's…I don't know, if I've just cuffed you to the bed and I'm between your legs eating you out until you have multiple orgas—can you still do that?"

Gabriel smirked. "Yes. Carry on."

"Fuck, I'm going to do that."

"Carry on!"

"Raincheck. But, yeah, when I'm doing that, I'm just using something to keep you still, or get you off, and there's no—I haven't forced you there, I've not been calling you a whore or forcing your legs open or hurting you…then okay, yes, scream my name to the ceiling so all your neighbours know who's fucking you, but *never, ever* when I'm being a bastard. Just — never. If it's anything that...I don't know, a random stranger could think 'that's abuse, that's rape, that's horrible', then don't."

Gabriel nodded. "I think I'll play it safe and not use it at all unless we're being soft-scoop-vanilla until I get more of an idea in practice."

"Please."

"Anything else?"

"I don't imagine this one will really apply to you, but I don't like doing things that will cause serious damage. Superficial stuff only. I watch the extreme porn, but again, it's just fantasies. So I might threaten to break your legs or something like that, but I will not, under any circumstances, cause deliberate damage to that level."

"Um, I'm not going to be asking you to break my legs."

"My wife did once," Aled said flatly, "and it shook me up for about a week that she'd even asked."

"Well, I'm going to throw a major fit if you even cause a cut big enough to need a single stitch, so I'm definitely not after any of that."

"Good," Aled said and kissed Gabriel's knuckles again. "We'll write it all down before we play anything, and we'll agree on some game to get us started, but — in time, you know, if it all goes well, you might...I don't know, get home to find I've broken in and I've got a bag over your head and your hands cuffed behind your back without telling you there's a game on. Don't want to play, safeword me. Want to play, just play along."

Gabriel's mouth twisted. "Traffic lights."

"Sorry?"

"Me and Kevin use traffic lights. Red is stop, just stop everything, game over, this is too much. Amber for stop *that*, or slow down, I need a breather, or I'm enjoying everything except that one thing you just did. Then there's green. And green is when *he* asks and I say I'm okay."

"Ah, so…surprise games, I can ask you for a colour?"

"Yeah. And if I say green, then I like it, let's go, I want to play and you might not get so worried later that you did anything wrong."

Aled smiled. "Thank you."

"Plus they're ingrained, so I'd default to them anyway."

"Then, we use them. I might have to drill into them a bit. Melissa used stop or checkmate."

"Um, no, I use stop when I don't mean stop. Just like no. I—you know, if we're playing a…a rape fantasy, or something, I'll be telling you to stop, but I don't really want you to. That's why Kevin came up with the traffic lights. I kept yelling stop and getting mad at him when he stopped."

Aled snorted with laughter.

"It was seriously a problem!" Gabriel whined.

"I can imagine. Okay. Traffic lights. That'll make me pause a bit at first, but I'll get used to it."

"Maybe just follow up a stop with a colour? Until you get used to it?"

Aled nodded. "Okay. Yeah. That could work."

"Aled, I have to ask…"

"Yeah?"

"You said outside of games, you don't want me to be submissive—"

"Yep."

"I'm pushy."

"What do you mean?"

"I'll sit on your lap and tell you to fuck me."

Aled laughed. "Feel free."

"But sometimes I won't want to play, especially if my body issues are acting up. But I won't want you to push and me to have to tell you, because it'll make me feel worse. So—if I'm wearing my boxers, I don't want to play. They're loose and comfortable and hide everything. They're my comfort underwear. I don't usually even want a fuck when I have boxers on. So they're a mute 'red', all right?"

"Got it," Aled said, toying lightly with Gabriel's nails. "God, you're fucking brilliant."

Gabriel blinked.

"You have this all figured out and you're telling me to fuck off about what I need to fuck off about—it's fantastic."

"Yeah?"

"Yeah. Like I said. I don't want a submissive. I want someone to *be* submissive when I want to get off, then to switch it off again. Like…well, I don't completely switch off the dominant thing, but I'm attracted to people who can and do tell me to get back in line when they've had enough. My wife was the most brilliant, clever woman I've ever met and I was in awe of her. And you, sitting there telling me to go fuck myself about drowning and shit—it's incredible."

Gabriel's smile was a little shy and Aled laughed, delighted with the dichotomy.

"God, there'll be some soft-scoop vanilla in a minute…"

"In a minute," Gabriel said, tugging on his hand. "Just one more thing."

"Go."

"You said silly movie date."

"What?"

"Earlier. When you were saying you didn't want me to be submissive except in scenes. You said you wanted silly movie dates and to laugh at people ice-skating. Is that what we are? Dating?"

Aled paused.

Were they?

Yes, his brain replied immediately.

"This — isn't just sex anymore, to me," he said slowly. "I'm attracted to you for more than sex. And I do — want, have, I think, a relationship with you."

"Aled —"

"I'm not saying you're my boyfriend," Aled interrupted quickly, squeezing Gabriel's caught hand between both of his. "I'm not saying I want to take you out to dinner all the time, and have you meet my nan, and be exclusive. I know you're not monogamous. I know that and I don't mind that. But I *am* attracted to you for more than just sex. Sometimes, I will want to just…come over, and watch movies, and eat popcorn with you. I want…that evening you covered my kitchen in cum and flour."

"The cum was all you, thank you very much."

"I want more of that," Aled said firmly. "This isn't meaningless sex. But I'm not staking any claim, either — I'm not really ready for a relationship and things are…complicated with me right now, with Melissa, so…I'm not staking any claim. I'm not going to be upset if you're sleeping with other men, I'm not going to assume I come first because I've caught a few feelings. Just…understand that sometimes, I'll text asking if you're free and it won't always be about getting your jeans off you in record time."

Gabriel nodded. "Okay. So long as we're clear."

"Want to try a game next weekend?"

Gabriel smiled. "Yeah, okay."

"Here?"

"Ah, no. Yours."

"Mine?" Aled frowned. "If it goes wrong…"

"Then I don't want the memory of a game gone wrong in my flat," Gabriel said firmly. "Yours or a hotel. Preferably yours so at least one of us knows what he's doing."

Aled nodded. "Okay. Mine. We'll write down all the rules and sort something out, but…later. This has been a bit heavy."

Gabriel looked a little relieved and Aled laughed.

"Not just me thinking it?"

"No."

"So—lunch? Find a cafe, people-watch, check out the cinema listings?"

"Is this one of your silly dates?"

Aled grinned, leaning right over the table to plant a smacker on Gabriel's lips.

"Yes," he said, "so let's get going."

Chapter Sixteen

Me: Can you come and pick me up from work?

That gang of teenagers had been loitering outside all day, throwing beer cans at passing cars and shouting. Gabriel felt stupid sometimes for being afraid of a bunch of kids, but other times they'd yell, "Oi, faggot!" and wolf-whistle him, and he figured it was perfectly justified.

Kevin: 10 minutes. You okay?

Me: Yeah, just them kids are hanging about again.

Kevin: Want to join us for dinner?

Me: I have to go and see Chris and Scott. I can get the bus.

Kevin: Don't be stupid, I'll drop you off. Judith's boxing up some lasagne for you.

Judith was an awesome cook and always gave him some leftovers. Gabriel hummed contentedly as he clocked out and went to loiter by the tills and talk to the new security guard. Bobby was tragically heterosexual, but he was friendly enough. They passed judgement on the crazy dog man who came in every Tuesday for a light bulb, two loaves of bread and a six pack of Diet — never regular — Pepsi. And eleven minutes later, the car cruised up out front and Kevin hit the horn.

The kids watched apprehensively. Kevin eyeballed them in return, looking like a Class A dealer with shotguns in the boot. He'd obviously been in the middle of something when Gabriel had texted, and was wearing jogging bottoms and a sweaty tank top. The interior of the car was humming a bit.

"Jesus," Gabriel complained. "You been working out in a dumpster?"

"Gardening."

"*Gardening?* Mind your image, tough man. Not sure it can take that."

Kevin snorted as he shoved the gearstick forward and the car lurched out of the parking area. "Hello to you, too, you catty little shit. You wanting a beating or something?"

Gabriel grinned. "Nah, I'm good."

"How you been?"

"Okay," he said. "Made up with Michael and got some texts from family asking for money again."

"Did you answer?"

"Did I fuck," Gabriel said, pulling a face. "And Aled and I talked about playing games and where we are and all that stuff."

"Go well?"

"Yep."

Kevin smirked. "I know that yep. Remember the rules."

"Yeah, yeah. Send you his postcode when I go for the first game."

"And nothing too crazy."

"He's not as crazy as you," Gabriel said. "Not by a long way."

"Doesn't have to be," Kevin returned. "Speaking of crazy, guess whose mother-in-law brought divorce paperwork and was trying to persuade Judith to fill it in?"

"Oh my God, she didn't..."

They bitched about families as they crawled through rush-hour traffic. Judith's family were well-heeled and hadn't liked Kevin from the start, even though they knew nothing about the whole kink aspect. They'd been even colder since Lily and Grace had arrived. Sometimes, Gabriel was grateful he'd lost touch with most of his family.

That was, except for Grandpa, Uncle Chris and Aunt Scott.

They lived in Pudsey. Aunt Scott owned a salon and Uncle Chris did something in IT. They had money. And with the money they had a fancy detached house in a cul-de-sac, with an annexe for Grandpa and a big back garden surrounded by thick trees. Sometimes Gabriel felt jealous—*look at that road, with no scuzzy kids or psychotic neighbours*—and other times he felt out of place and uncomfortable. Kinky round there meant a can of whipped cream and a DVD of softcore porn. Being dropped off by Kevin felt sleazy all on its own.

"Give us a ring if you need picking up again," Kevin said and beckoned. Gabriel rolled his eyes but kissed him goodbye, then rummaged in his pocket for a key and let himself in.

He'd lived here, briefly. After things had fallen through with Jim, he'd been twenty years old and homeless in Sheffield. He'd spent his last cash on a train ticket and just turned up at Uncle Chris and Aunt Scott's door.

They were the only family who'd have helped, after all.

The house never changed. Aunt Scott was the fastidious type. Same mat. Same peaches-and-cream colour scheme. Even the same ugly cat. She was called Snowball, but Gabriel called her Snotbag. She had a face like she'd been twatted with a brick. Repeatedly. She flounced off at the sight of him and he stuck his tongue out at her like a little kid before taking off his shoes.

"Chris! Scott!" A pause. "Grandpa?"

To his surprise, a creaking voice told him off for shouting and Gabriel followed it into the study.

"Sorry, Grandpa. How you doing?"

He offered a hug. Grandpa scowled and called him a nancy.

"Love you, too," Gabriel said breezily. "How have you been? Did the hospital make that eye appointment for you?"

"Bloody good-for-nothing doctors. I'm fine!" Grandpa snapped. He seized Gabriel's jaw in clawed fingers and turned his face this way and that, examining. "You've got whiskers. You look like a scruff. Learn to shave."

Gabriel laughed. "All right, Grandpa."

It was a long way from where they'd started. When he'd come out—all of twelve years old and stupid, utterly stupid for believing for a minute that his family were going to love him anyway—his grandfather had simply said, "No." They hadn't spoken again until Gabriel was twenty-two and Grandpa had moved in with Uncle Chris.

And he'd just said, *'Long time no see, boy.'*

They'd never discussed it. But somewhere in the intervening decade, in which Gabriel hadn't known if Grandpa was dead or alive—or vice versa, he imagined—he had transformed from an unacceptable stain to a tolerated grandson.

"Make yourself useful," Grandpa said, waving his stick at a stack of old newspapers by his chair. "Get rid of those."

"Okay."

It was the main reason that Gabriel visited every month. Grandpa was slowing down. He couldn't so much as walk round the corner shop anymore. His hearing had deteriorated to the point where the hearing aids didn't help. His hands shook on the head of the cane and it took him a good three minutes to get up out of his armchair. And if Uncle Chris and Aunt Scott were out all day, Grandpa couldn't eat. He couldn't open boxes or packets or bottles of milk.

So every few weeks, Gabriel would come over so his aunt and uncle could have a break.

He cleaned out some rubbish, then helped his grandfather get from the study to the kitchen. They didn't talk much. Grandpa read the paper while Gabriel cooked, and grumbled about the news. Gabriel just agreed in the right places.

It felt—

Weird. Honestly, it felt weird. He'd run away from home at sixteen. He wasn't used to playing happy families. He had felt out of place and uncomfortable in this fancy house from the moment he'd moved in and for all the noise Uncle Chris had made about him staying and saving up for a mortgage, Gabriel had had no intention of doing so. The flats were vile, the neighbourhood grotty, the local kids a nightmare — but it was what he was used to. It was home.

Shredding kale to the instructions in Aunt Scott's cookbook wasn't.

But they had taken him in after things in Sheffield had collapsed and Gabriel still carried the gratitude around with him. So, if him turning up once a month to make dinner and put Grandpa to bed would let Uncle Chris and Aunt Scott have a date night, who was he to argue?

"Turn that damn thing off!" Grandpa snapped when his mobile buzzed on the table and Gabriel rescued it before it could come to harm.

"It's just—"

Aled: Busy?

"My partner, Grandpa," he said quickly.

"Partner?" Grandpa's eyes narrowed. "Don't tell me you're a nancy like these two."

Me: Making dinner for my grumpy old fart of a grandfather! What you up to?

"Always have been," he said casually, knowing better than to take the old git seriously.

Aled: Ahh, no sexting then?

Me: Not right now ;)

"Tell him to piss off and find a proper girl!"

Me: Grandpa says hi.

Aled: Hey, Gabriel's grandpa.

"Aled says hi."
"Pansy."
Gabriel snorted with laughter. Maybe he ought to have invited Kevin in after all. That would have just about killed Grandpa stone dead.

Aled: Didn't think you'd have family round here, not with your accent.

Me: My uncle married a Yorkshire boy. Lives in Pudsey. They look after Grandpa now.

"You need to find a woman," Grandpa said decisively, folding up the paper with shaking, swollen fingers as the timer went off. "Find yourself a nice wife. Have some kids."

"Not exactly got the plumbing for that," Gabriel said, hefting the tray out of the oven. It was undercooked, just the way the weird old man liked it. "Anyway, I'm not into women."

"Stuff and nonsense. You don't marry someone because you're into them! You find yourself someone who can cook and clean and raise a few babies. You don't have to like them."

"God, Grandpa, are you sure you weren't born in the wrong century? You'd fit right into the thirteenth, you know."

Aled: That's nice of them :)

Me: Yeah well my mum can't look after a goldfish so it was that or a care home nobody can afford.

Aled: My nan's in a care home. She'd like you.

Gabriel raised his eyebrows.

Me: My own nana didn't like me.

Aled: Well mine would. She likes anyone who makes fun of me.

Me: Oh sold! ;)

"Stop flirting and get that on the plates."

"Yes, Grandpa."

Me: I might have told him you're my partner.

Aled: If he's anything like my nana he'll forget in a bit.

Me: Probably. Long as he doesn't tell my uncle.

Aled: Mother's brother? Father's?

Me: Mum's, No dad. Lots of brothers and sisters though.

Aled: Only child :(

Gabriel winced. He *wished*. God, he'd have given anything to be an only child. From his eldest brother trying to drown him in the bath for being a freak when he came out, to his youngest sister and that incident with the kettle — yeah, only child beat middle punching bag every time.

Aled: I was texting for a reason, actually.

Me: Yeah, you said, sexting.

Aled: Nope.

Me: Boring. Go away then. Come back when you have dick pics.

Aled: Charming. Was going to ask if you want to come over on Saturday for a game?

Me: Working. Sunday?

Aled: Sunday it is x

Me: Going to tell me what we're playing?

There was a long, long pause.
Then he realised he'd landed himself a sadist, when Aled sent his reply.

Aled: Why spoil the surprise?

Chapter Seventeen

"Gabriel and I had the talk."

Aled said it the moment that Suze sank into the hydrotherapy pool next to him and she rolled her eyes.

"Oh good," she said tartly. "Does he know where babies come from now?"

"Sod off."

"What talk?"

"The boundaries talk."

Her grumpy face eased and she smiled, although Aled reflected that it might be more to do with the jets and the hot water than his news.

"So you're going to start playing with him?"

"Soon. He's coming over tomorrow."

"Were you right? He's done this before?"

"Yeah. He's good, too, he knew what he wants and what he doesn't, and he wasn't shy about telling me what wasn't allowed."

"Which is?"

"Nothing too surprising. There's a bit of a grey area around what I'm allowed to say during scenes with regards to his vagina, but—"

Suze choked on her protein shake. "I'm sorry, his *what?*"

Aled blinked. "His vagina."

"He doesn't have a vagina!"

"Uh, yes, he definitely does. I've been inside it," Aled said slowly.

"But he's a man!"

Aled frowned. "It was on his Grindr profile."

"I barely remember your birthday, never mind what profiles you were looking at. He has a *vagina?*"

"Well...yeah. He's transgender," Aled said, then frowned harder. Was he even supposed to tell people? "Er, I have no idea if I'm allowed to tell you that, so—"

"Well, I'm not going to say anything," Suze said blankly, then blinked owlishly at him. "So he's—you know—what's there when you get his kit off?"

Aled bit his lip. The answer of *biggest clit you've ever seen* was on the tip of his tongue, but something felt off about just...well, laughing about Gabriel's anatomy when he wasn't even here. "I don't know I should be talking about it."

"Have you got a picture of him?"

"No," Aled admitted.

"Get one. Does he look girly?"

"We really shouldn't be talking about this."

"Oh, come on! Is he shorter than you, then? He must be if he's a g—a trans."

"Trans. Not 'a trans'. And not by much. Couple of inches, tops. Five foot six, at least."

"You're only five seven."

"Well, there you go."

Suze frowned.

"Come on, Suze, don't be a dick about it."

"I'm not!" she protested, hitting him. "I'm just surprised, is all. I thought you'd be off women for ages after — well, after."

"Trust me, he might have the equipment, but he's no woman," Aled said significantly.

"Built?"

"Nah, wiry. But he's fit. Cycles everywhere."

"Urgh, he's a nutjob, dump him."

"He does have his down sides —"

They laughed in unison, then Suze pulled a face. "Sorry," she said. "That was rude of me."

"A bit."

"I'm sure he's lovely. And hey, it's not like you're gay and haven't a clue what to do with his, uh…"

"Original plumbing?"

"Nice," Suze said approvingly. "I like that. Original plumbing. Does he have it all?"

"Suze!"

"You need to know that!"

"Why?" Aled asked. "Not like I could get him pregnant."

Suze smirked and slid farther down in the water until her chin touched the surface.

"So he's kinky and sex mad and you can't knock him up?"

"Basically."

"You're lucky," she said wistfully. "A sex-mad fuckbuddy. I need to bribe mine with clean socks and bacon sandwiches before he'll unglue himself from the rugby long enough to fuck me. And he only takes six minutes from start to finish."

Aled cracked a smile, and another joke, but his mind wandered off. He *was* lucky. He had a new submissive, one who was fun and gorgeous and brilliant, and would be bound to keep Aled on his toes.

And who, potentially, could become more than an outlet and a plaything. Who could become —

Vital.

* * * *

Aled stayed late at the gym, long after Suze had gone home to bribe her boyfriend with bacon sandwiches. He soaked in the hydrotherapy pool for nearly an hour before having a go on a treadmill for a while to at least try to curb the spread of his belly, and by the time he left, night had well and truly fallen and his car stood almost alone.

Almost.

"Oh shit."

Parked right next to it was Melissa's old yellow contraption and Aled swore under his breath as he approached. She was waiting by his passenger door, arms folded, and he didn't need to see her face to know that she was angry and they were about to have an unholy row.

"Melissa. How are —"

"Stop ignoring the paperwork, Aled," she said tightly. "I've dropped you two copies now."

"I know," Aled said. "But I don't —"

"You don't want to sign it."

"Of course I don't! You're my wife!"

"Not anymore!" she shouted and Aled flinched back as though she'd slapped him. "This is over, Aled! We can't work around the stalemate and I've — I've found someone else, and I want to be with him, and have a family, and I can't do that if I'm still married to you!"

"We never talked about it, we never —"

"We talked plenty and I am done talking," she said tightly. "Sign the paperwork, Aled. Let go."

"I'm not ready to let go."

"How long do you want? It's been a year, Aled. I've moved on and you ought to as well."

"How am I supposed to move on from you?" Aled implored. "I love you, Melissa. I've always loved you, I'm always going to love you, I —"

"But I don't."

She near-whispered it and Aled stopped short. A lump formed in his throat, solid and painful, and she looked away.

"I don't, Aled. Not anymore. And I don't want this to get nasty, I don't want to do that, I've every intention of just getting the divorce and walking away. I will not take your money or your house, I will not contest any of it or ask for anything, but I *need* that divorce. And if you try to stop it, I *will* take you to court for everything. *Everything.* So please don't make me do that."

Aled shook his head numbly. "You're my wife."

"And I walked away. So let me keep walking."

"So you can fuck some other man and have his kids," Aled said harshly, a sudden wash of anger rising up through his stomach and chest. "Is that all I was ever worth to you, a cock who could give you k —"

She slapped him.

For a moment, there was silence.

Then Aled got in his car. She hit the window, shouting his name, but he simply turned the engine over and put his foot down, his tyres spinning for a moment as they fought for purchase. His fingers were shaking on the wheel and he felt sick and angry. For a brief moment, he'd wanted to hit her back. He'd wanted to hurt her. He'd wanted her to understand how he felt, because she clearly didn't feel the same. How easy had it been for her to walk away from him? How quickly had she replaced him, with that fucking colleague who'd always fancied her? Had they been screwing *before* she left, or —

Aled shook his head, trying to displace the thought. No. Melissa wasn't a cheat. She wouldn't have done that to him.

But then, once, he would have said she wouldn't have left him.

He drove mindlessly, out through Ossett before turning the car north, then paused and pulled over. The hypocrisy in his own words was getting loud as they replayed in his head. He loved her, but he was fucking Gabriel. He didn't want to move on, but he had a new relationship. He wanted to be with her — but he wanted to be with someone else.

He needed her.

But —

Did he *want* her?

He couldn't go to Gabriel. Not so angry, and so soon after establishing their boundaries. He'd make a mistake, come in too heavy and too frightening. He'd fuck it up.

But fuck, he *needed* —

He needed to punish someone. He needed to get out this sudden anger — and alien anger, because he'd never been angry at her before. He'd never hated her for walking and yet suddenly, he *did*. Suddenly, he wanted to — to —

He dropped his head back against the steering wheel and unzipped his jeans. Fuck. If he couldn't actually use Gabriel, he could still make use of him. He fumbled for his phone and found Gabriel's number with one hand while beginning to stroke himself with the other. If he couldn't physically fuck it out, he could get close.

"Hello?"

"You home?"

"Yeah."

"Alone?"

"Yeah. You want to come over?"

"Can't," Aled croaked. "Too angry. I won't be able to control myself."

"Angry? What's—"

"If you were here," Aled interrupted harshly, "I'd use you and fuck it out. You're not, but I'm going to do that anyway. What are you wearing?"

Gabriel's voice dropped at least an octave. "White T-shirt, tartan pyjama bottoms. No shoes. Briefs."

"I could come and pick you up," Aled whispered, massaging his cock, "and I'd drive you out somewhere quiet, where we wouldn't be interrupted. Where nobody would hear you."

"I wouldn't want to," Gabriel whispered. "You'd hurt me, if you were angry."

"You'd resist me?"

"I'd offer you something else, maybe a—"

"I want to fuck you until you're begging me to stop," Aled grunted, beginning to thrust into his palm. His cock was steel-hard and hot in his fingers, straining for somewhere to go. "And if you resist me, I'll only hold you down and fuck you anyway. You're a slave to cock and slaves don't get to say no."

"I'd try anyway," Gabriel whispered. Aled could hear the soft rustle of cloth, then Gabriel's breathing changed. "I'd fight you."

"I'd drag you out of the car by the throat and hold you down over the bonnet. The metal's hot. Engine's running. You'll be pushing back up into me to get away from it and I'd tell you to pull your pyjamas down."

"I wouldn't do it."

"Then I'd do it for you. Just far enough to shove my cock inside." Aled squeezed, a poor imitation of the way Gabriel would clench and shudder around him, and closed his eyes. "You'd be crying. Completely dry, it'll hurt. You'll feel like I've stuck you, like I've broken you open from the inside. Only you can only snap someone once. I'd make sure to fuck you deep, balls-deep, so you feel every last inch of me, so you can't get away…"

Gabriel whined, a high, keening noise.

"If you yell, if you try and call for help, I'd hold my hand over your mouth to keep you quiet, and I'd thrust even harder. Full weight on your back. The metal would burn you, but that'll be nothing compared to the pain when I shoot my load and there's blood and semen leaking down your thighs."

"Oh *God* – "

"I'd pull out and pull your clothes back up, then I'd shove you in the back seat. Child locks, you see. I'd tie your hands behind your back with my belt, because when I'm angry, I always want more than one fuck. I'd drive us back to your flat and I'll park us up in the street. But you don't get to go until you've satisfied me and one bonnet fuck isn't going to cut it. So what are you going to do, to get to go home?"

"I – "

Gabriel's voice was shuddering and Aled's chest heaving. His balls were tightening.

Fuck, come on, Gabriel, satisfy me.

"I'd offer to jack you off, but that wouldn't be enough for you, you want inside, you want to spread my legs and hurt me, humiliate me, so you'd come in the backseat and turn me over, you'd pull my pyjamas down again and you'd sit there, looking at me, taunting me, while your fingers are — are twisting inside me, you're finger-fucking me and asking me if — if I think my job's done when you're hard again. I'd try and close my legs and I'd tell you no, so you — you slap me, you call me a selfish whore and you shove your cock inside me, you're pinning me under your weight and you're holding your hand on my mouth again, telling me to open my eyes and look at you, I'm looking at you, and you're hurting me, you're thrusting so hard it hurts, you're too big and it hurts and you don't care, you're telling me to shut up and enjoy it — "

Aled came hard with a guttural groan, his orgasm coating his hand and the bottom of the steering wheel, his feet scrabbling against the footwell. Gabriel's voice was fading out, shaking badly, and Aled laughed, staring blindly at the roof of the car.

"Of course I do, because you do enjoy it," he whispered. "I'm holding you down and fucking you open and all I'd have to do is lick my seed back out of you when I'm done and you'd be coming on my tongue like a slut — "

Gabriel gasped and an incoherent cry said he'd found his own climax. Aled breathed through it, massaging his softened cock and imagining Gabriel's face in the darkness of the car.

"Fuck," Gabriel whispered. "Fuck, are you *sure* you're too angry to come over?"

"Sorry," Aled said quietly. "I'd overstep the mark. But soon. I—I don't know about tomorrow. But soon."

"*Very* soon. Promise?"

"Promise. And thanks, sweetheart."

"Fuck you and your thanks," Gabriel groaned. "I just had the best wank of my life and you're refusing to come over and give me an amazing fuck to go with it. That's not thanks."

Aled smiled, tucking himself back into his jeans, and exhaled. "Soon," he promised again. "Maybe even tomorrow, if I calm down. Just…not now."

"Okay," Gabriel said quietly, then paused. "Aled?"

"Mm?"

"When soon comes…bring a belt."

Chapter Eighteen

Gabriel wasn't impressed.

He'd been promised a game on Sunday—then something had ticked Aled off and it had been cancelled at the last minute. Gabriel appreciated the thoughtfulness, and the self-awareness of where the line was on Aled's part was hugely reassuring, but—

But.

He'd been promised kinky sex. And he'd got no sex at all.

Grace had colic, so Kevin was in no mood for games—or at least not a mood Gabriel wanted unleashing anywhere near his backside. Michael had a dick like a baseball bat, but he was so boring—shove it in, jizz, pack up and go—that it would be more frustrating than anything else. And Gabriel wasn't in the mood for new guys goggling at a vagina like they'd never seen one before.

He wanted Aled. Even if it wasn't the promised game.

So on Wednesday, he packed an overnight bag, called in sick to work and caught a bus. Then another. Then walked a bit. And, finding the driveway empty, got out a packet of fags, sat down on the doorstep and had a smoke while he waited. He was going to get *something*. Even if it was just getting on his knees on the doormat and blowing Aled as a welcome home greeting.

The street was surprisingly busy. Gabriel didn't really know Wakefield all that well and his initial impression of it being a bit of a fancy road was wrong. A couple of builders working on the house opposite kept staring at him. There were a couple of scabby ten-year-olds riding bikes around in the road, shouting like they were at a rock concert. It wasn't exactly Belle Isle level, but it wasn't Uncle Chris' quiet cul-de-sac either.

He was in the middle of a game on his phone when the car pulled up. It just *appeared,* swinging up off the road like it was about to go into the side of the house. Gabriel jumped, then grinned at the startled look Aled gave him when he got out.

"Er, hi?"

"Hi!" Gabriel said brightly.

"Not that I'm not pleased to see you, but what are you doing here?"

"I fancied a night with you," Gabriel said, kicking his bag. "You scammed me out of a game on Sunday, so I'm all frustrated."

Aled snorted. "My wife did. And I'm not — kink's not a good idea right now."

"Still in a temper?"

"Yeah."

"That's okay," Gabriel said, standing up when Aled came to unlock the door. "We can just make brownies again or something."

When the front door closed behind them, hands fisted in Gabriel's jacket and hauled him to his tiptoes. Aled's mouth nudged his own briefly before a dangerous whisper slipped free between them.

"You want me to eat you out on the floor again, do you?"

"Um—"

"You're taking liberties."

"How about this," Gabriel murmured, tucking his fingers into the top of Aled's suit trousers. "You're a hardworking guy. You've been busting a nut at the office all day. Why shouldn't you come home to a thank you?"

Aled's mouth quirked against his own—and the hands relaxed. One slid around to cup the back of Gabriel's neck. The kiss was softer. Open, but somehow chaste. Sweet again and Gabriel found himself clutching at the lapels of Aled's suit jacket in return.

"It's really not a good idea," Aled said gently. "But I would appreciate some company."

"Deal."

Aled seemed...not depressed, exactly, but down in the dumps. He was subdued. Gabriel put the effort in to cheering him up, shooing him off for a hot shower and raiding the kitchen for ingredients to make assorted goodies. He found a toad-in-the-hole recipe and the right things and destroyed half the cutlery and panware. But successfully. By the time Aled came back down, in a very old university hoodie and a pair of jogging bottoms with a hole in the seat, the kitchen was filled with a delicious smell and Gabriel was sitting cross-legged on the floor, watching the sausage-stuffed Yorkshire pudding rise.

"What did you *do*?"

"I cooked!"

"And you're going to be cleaning," Aled said.

"It's toad-in-the-hole. You can't complain about toad-in-the-hole."

"I'm supposed to be watching my weight," Aled muttered.

"Only if it's cutting off my air," Gabriel replied loftily and grinned up at him from the floor. "You want to start a movie while this finishes?"

"You really don't want to know?"

"Know what?"

"Why I had to cancel Sunday?"

Gabriel shrugged. "I figured if you wanted to talk about it, you would. Do you?"

"Not really."

"Then I don't care," he said. "Honestly, I kind of appreciate that you know when you shouldn't be playing."

Aled grunted. He levered himself down on the floor beside Gabriel, leaning his back against the cabinets.

"I usually don't have much of a temper," he said. "Suze calls me mild-mannered. But when I do go —"

"Stereotypical ginger?"

"Oh, fuck off."

Gabriel laughed and nuzzled at Aled's jaw. "Sorry."

"No, you're not."

"Not really," Gabriel agreed. He looped his arms around Aled's neck and slid over his thigh to straddle it. "I can't really see you getting angry, to be honest. You do intense well, but I don't know about angry."

Aled smirked. Gabriel caught the corner of it with his mouth and chewed. He could feel a soft pressure between his legs and captured the tiny grunt when he rocked his hips over it.

"You want me?"

"Usually do."

"I have an idea."

"What?"

"I'll show you after dinner."

A hand smacked his arse. "Tease."

Aled mock-sulked until dinner was ready, then Gabriel was subjected to an hour of some awful programme on SyFy.

"This is why I don't bother with a media package," he commented as a girl in a latex jumpsuit lay down in a giant fish tank, sans fish. "You don't get this garbage on the free stuff."

"No, you get *Antiques Roadshow* instead."

"I've been fucked to *Antiques Roadshow*. It's not bad."

"Whoever was doing you had a weird fetish then."

"Eh, you're not wrong—*what* is she doing?"

It was awful. But there was cookie dough ice cream in the freezer, so they split a tub and Gabriel tried to figure out why the fish tank was needed to go rummaging around in people's brains. At least the genius friend was kind of cute.

"They're all cute," Aled opined.

"Too many X chromosomes."

"You're gay, then?"

"As a morris dancer."

Aled chuckled, taking the empty tub back into the kitchen. When he came back, Gabriel fully expected the arm back over his shoulders and another episode of *Pretty People Go Brain Combing* or whatever the show was actually called.

What he got was kissed.

Hard.

It wasn't a coax, a flirt or even a seduction. It was a hand gripping his jaw and a mouth sealed over his. The invasion was immediate and intense and he sagged back into the cushions, spellbound.

"You had an idea," Aled whispered, nosing at his ear.

"Um—y-yeah…"

"Tell me."

Gabriel blinked. "Uh. Okay. Um. Give me your hoodie."

Aled raised his eyebrows but leaned back and took it off. He was wearing a T-shirt underneath. White. Bland. Vanilla.

And okay, what Gabriel had in mind wasn't kink. But it wasn't total milk, either.

He stripped wordlessly and without trying to make it sexy either. Aled's gaze raked him all the same. And when Gabriel put the hoodie on—so large on him that it made a modest dress—he saw the spark light in Aled's eyes.

"Kneel down."

Gabriel blinked at the dark purr and knelt almost on instinct. Aled leaned forward. For a moment, Gabriel thought he was going to have his head pulled down onto cock, but instead, Aled pulled up the hood, and took hold of the sleeves.

And knotted them.

Behind Gabriel's head.

Hard.

Gabriel tugged and the sleeves refused to give. Aled smirked, then took him by the elbows and pulled him back up onto the sofa. In a moment, Gabriel was surrounded. Invaded. He was on his back, arms tied behind his neck, Aled nuzzling at his jaw and preventing his elbows from closing.

And his naked lower half bracketed Aled's hips as though they were already mid-fuck.

Matthew J. Metzger

It was—

Vulnerable. He was pushed deep into the sofa. Aled was all around him—an arm under his back, holding the knot in the sleeves so Gabriel couldn't free himself. Hips between his thighs, pushing them open and rubbing his pussy on the cotton of Aled's jogging bottoms, chest bearing down on Gabriel's until there was no hope of movement. A hand moved between them. Teeth gnawed at his jaw.

Then it wasn't cotton, but cock. And the hand between them had moved to grip Gabriel's hair, forcing his mouth against Aled's. And he was groaning around Aled's tongue, as he was slowly, achingly, deliberately parted by a painfully dry, agonisingly thick, desperately needed dick.

It didn't stay dry long.

The flood of arousal was so intense Gabriel wondered for a split second if he'd wet himself. But then Aled held his jaw open and kissed him, as messy as his cock as it slid free. Then cock and tongue invaded all the same time, and Gabriel—

He existed for this.

For Aled to slide his cock into. For Aled to steal the air from. He was trapped, tangled up in cotton and cushion. His upper body was shielded by the hoodie, but who needed that? It was his cunt that was needed.

"Harder."

It escaped in a breathy whisper. Aled's chest left his own. An arm braced that weight. Hips rose—and the next thrust *plunged*. Deeper. Harder. He couldn't spread his legs wide enough. He couldn't fuck back. And he didn't need to. It ached. It almost hurt. The drag of steel dick against the smooth wetness inside him—it wasn't a screw, or a shag, or any kind of love. It was a plunder. A hammer. A *fuck*.

"Fuck-fuck-fuck-fuck—"

He tipped his hips up. Caught the very edge of Aled's hair and skin. Began to rub himself off on Aled's belly—

Then two hands forced his hips back down to the sofa.

"You'll get your turn."

"Oh, *fuck*—!"

He didn't need anything else.

It just happened. Like that. The rough command. The denial. The pecking—pegging?—order. Aled would fuck all he wanted and Gabriel could come later, when it was his turn.

Only he didn't.

He came then and there, on the dick splitting him open from the lips up, and to hell with the pegging order.

The world—

He blinked.

Vision came back together like pixels recrystallising. The cock inside was moving harder, faster, deeper. His hips were being slammed down onto it. He'd have bruises. Fingerprints. He could hear Aled swearing under his breath. He was close. So damn close—

"Fill me," Gabriel breathed

Aled kissed him.

Then—

Pulled out.

Just like that, his dick was gone. Gabriel blinked at the sudden emptiness. His pussy gaped. Cold. Hollow.

Hands. Cushions. A slap on one arse cheek that made him yowl.

Then that hot, wet cock pushing right back up into him like it belonged. Filling him up once more. He sighed and rocked his arse up into Aled's hips. Relaxed into the sofa under his cheek. *Belonged.*

"You want to fuck yourself on the cushions, be my guest," came the low, filthy whisper in his ear. Weight settled all along his back. Two fingers pushed past his lips and hooked behind his bottom front teeth. "But keep your mouth busy. You'll be cleaning it later."

Gabriel whined.

Then sucked.

Then was fucked.

And it wasn't in the least bit vanilla.

Chapter Nineteen

Aled opened the door and groaned. "No."

"Yep," Tom said. "Get your coat, I'm buying."

"Oh, you're buying?"

"Yes."

"All evening?"

"Yes."

Aled eyed him, then shrugged. "Fine."

Turned out, Tom had a specific destination and purpose in mind—a bar crawl in Leeds. Still, drinking in Leeds was stupidly expensive, and worse so on a Friday night, so Aled didn't overly argue, and only said he'd known it was a trap all along when Suze joined them.

"Well, you might be seeing this Gabriel a bit more, or you might be lying to me and still wallowing, so I thought we'd best play it safe and drag you out anyway," she said cheerfully and raised her glass. "Cheers."

"Fuck you both," Aled decided and downed half of his pint. "I'm going to get wasted if Tom's buying."

"Hang on a minute —"

"You said all night. It's a binding contract."

Tom sulked. Suze laughed at him and joined Aled in drinking herself under the table. Truth be told, Aled felt grateful for the offer. The divorce paperwork was haunting his kitchen, making him strangely reluctant to even go in there, and his idea of inviting Gabriel over for that long-promised game had been vetoed by Gabriel having plans. Some party or other.

So for once, Tom and Suze's plan of getting him out of the house by getting him wasted was welcome.

"To friends and their wallets," he decided, raising his glass.

They stopped in three bars before Aled would have said he was tipsy, then found a pub near the train station to get resoundingly wankered. It was nearing ten o'clock when Suze turned the conversation to the divorce, and ten-oh-two when Aled steered it firmly away again.

Or tried to, because Suze simply jabbed her finger at him and said, "You haven't signed the papers, have you?"

"I *don't* want to talk about it."

"Tough." God, she was persistent. "Sign them."

"Maybe I've not signed them because I don't want to?"

"You still love her?"

"You know I —"

"Then sign them and let her do what she wants, that's what you do when you love someone."

"It's not that easy —"

"I'm getting another drink!" Tom announced loudly. Aled asked for an entire bottle of whisky, but Suze wasn't allowing him any escape.

"Focus! Sign them."

"I don't want to bloody well sign them. If I sign them, it's over."

"It's over anyway. For Christ's sake, you're obviously taken with this new guy. Just let Melissa go and —"

"And what, admit that I can't even stick to a marriage vow? Admit I let everyone down?"

"She's to blame as much as y —"

"That doesn't matter."

Suze's eyes narrowed. "Aled, you can't possibly mean your *dad*, can you?"

"He held on long enough to see me get married, Suze. He said so himself. He said it was — it was the proudest fucking moment of his life, watching me and Melissa get hitched. Said it meant his job as my dad was done, only —"

Aled's voice cracked. Only, of course, that was never true. Dads weren't expendable like that. Their jobs didn't just end like that.

Their lives, though —

"Oh, honey."

"I *promised*, Suze. In front of you and her and my dad. In front of everyone who's most important to me. And if I sign those papers, I'm *breaking* that promise."

"Not to Melissa," Suze said softly. "Not to me. And, sweetheart, if your dad could see you now, he'd *never* tell you that you failed him. He was proud because he saw you so *happy* that day and he figured you'd be all right after he'd gone, now you'd made a new family of your own. That's all. Your dad never, not *ever*, would have wanted you to feel like you'd failed him by getting a divorce."

And there was the truth of it. Right there. It wasn't her. It hadn't been her since Gabriel had wriggled his way into Aled's life and bed. It had been *Dad*.

It had been the divorce itself. He loved her, but he'd never been the type to try to stop her. He'd never tried to stop her walking away. He'd never tried to make her give up her affairs with the other men. He'd never tried to be the one and only, even when they'd gotten married — and at the end of the day, he'd never tried to stop her falling in love with someone else.

But he was trying to stop the divorce.

He was trying to avoid *being* divorced.

Aled shook his head, the tears blurring his voice, and felt Suze's narrow fingers clasp around his wrist. For a split second, he hated her. He hated her truth and the way she cut through the bullshit and the hypocrisy. It was easier, wasn't it? It was easier to pretend it was all about loving Melissa, and nothing to do with failing his father.

Nothing to do with failing.

"Aled." Her voice was so soft it was barely audible. "You will fail your dad if, and only if, you fail to live up to your full potential. If you fail to be the man he foresaw you being. And your dad saw you as an honest, clever, kind, generous man. Not as somebody's husband or someone's father. Just *you*. You've never once failed him, sweetheart, I promise you."

Aled closed his eyes and gripped her hand until his fingers stopped shaking.

Then Tom crashed in, slamming pints on the table and bellowing, "Fuck this malarkey, let's get wankered!"

Aled laughed throatily as Suze huffed and hit her boyfriend, and took his pint, grateful for the reprieve.

His chest ached thinking about his late father, as it always did, and he downed half the pint to hide the tremor in his jaw.

"Sign the papers, be single, come out and get hammered, fuck a bunch of blokes and find a pretty girl," Tom instructed, then grinned. "Or a pretty bloke. Can't look like your ex, though, that's bad karma."

"I don't want to talk about her," Aled said, nearly spilling the remnants of his pint. "If we want to talk about my love life, then we can talk about Gabriel."

"Your Grindr guy?" Tom said. "The transsexy one?"

"Transgender," Aled said tightly.

"S'what I said. Transsexy. Does he actually?"

Aled scowled. "Does he what?"

"Have both," Tom said. "I mean, like, can you fuck him like a girl?"

Aled stiffened. Something crawled under his skin, cold and angry. "He's not a girl," he said tensely. "Trust me. He's not."

"Yeah, but he *was* – "

"Tom, shut up," Suze snapped.

"I'm just *asking*. You shagged him again?" Tom asked.

"Several times."

"You what? Several? Are you dating?"

Aled pursed his lips. "Yeah. I guess we are. We're playing."

"Playing? What the fuck is – "

"I can tie him up and fuck him with a broom handle if I want," Aled said, too loudly, and Tom went scarlet.

"Oh, for fuck's sake!" he moaned, clapping his hands over his ears. "What is it with you and your kinky mates, Suze?"

"How is this my fault?" she protested.

"You were trying to get me in handcuffs the other night, and now —"

"Whoa, I do not want to imagine that," Aled said, draining his glass. "You have your domestic. I need a piss."

He staggered up from the table, the room lurching, and swayed his way out — not to the toilets, but outside. He needed a few minutes to himself. The pub was crowded and dark, full of shadowy people, and far too hot — but the cold air outside hit him like a brick in the face and he raked in a deep lungful of polluted air like he'd been imprisoned for a thousand years. He threw out his arms, nearly knocking someone off the pavement, and did it again.

"How drunk are you?" a voice asked.

Aled snorted at a helicopter wheeling by overhead. "Not drunk enough."

"You seem pretty drunk."

"Might look like this sober."

"You don't."

"How do you —" Aled started, then looked down into Gabriel's smirking gaze. "Holy shit."

Gabriel grinned. "You here with Tom and Suze?"

"Yeah. You?"

"On my way to a club to find someone to do," Gabriel said and the grin widened. "But maybe I found someone early?"

Aled grinned. He ducked in for a kiss, but Gabriel darted aside and it landed on his cheek.

"Come back to mine?" he asked.

"Yours? Mine is closer."

"I have a train ticket and we can get you one, too. Last one's just after ten. Come and sit with us. Tom's buying."

"Not sure I want to wait until ten," Gabriel coaxed, fingers toying with the fly on Aled's jeans.

"Stalls?"

"No thanks. Pubs. Bad idea. I'll come say hi quickly, though."

Aled laughed. "Okay." He caught Gabriel's hand and tugged him towards the door. "Come and meet them. You never met them. Then we'll go and get the train."

In the maybe four minutes he'd been outside, the pub had got impossibly busier. Aled hooked his fingers into Gabriel's belt loops and towed him firmly back towards the table, grinning when Suze raised her eyebrows at them, and presented Gabriel like a gift, hands gripping his shoulders. "It's him."

"Hello," Gabriel said.

"Who's 'him'?" Suze asked, but Tom's face had lit up in a grin.

"The Grindr guy," he said too loudly and raised his glass. "Cheers to the bloke who can put a smile on that miserable bastard's face."

Gabriel laughed. "Aled's a miserable bastard?"

"Fucking awful," Tom confirmed. "Hey, I got a question—"

"No," Aled interrupted sharply and Gabriel frowned, half-turning to look at him, but Tom was too drunk and it was too late.

"Do you fuck like a girl?"

Gabriel stiffened. His shoulders tightened between Aled's palms and Aled scowled. "Tom—"

"Ignore him," Suze said sharply. "Just ignore him, he's had way too much—"

"I've not, I'm *asking*, I'm allowed to *ask*—"

"You're being a twat!"

"I don't do anything like a girl," Gabriel retorted, too harshly, and Aled tugged him back from the table.

"I'm kidnapping you," he said, rubbing his jaw against Gabriel's ear. "C'mon, let me kidnap you."

Gabriel shrugged him off, pulling away a little bit, and Aled frowned, suddenly uncertain. Suze was scolding Tom — who was still protesting his innocence to Suze and claiming that if Gabriel had a cunt, then he was a she — and Aled grimaced.

Shit.

Time to bail — and preferably *with* Gabriel, if he wanted to not let Tom and his complete lack of brains ruin this newfound fling.

"Hey," he mumbled, pulling Gabriel back by the shoulders, away from the table. "Ignore him. Come home with me?"

Gabriel twisted away again, but this time caught Aled's wrist and pulled him towards the door. Aled allowed himself to be towed out into the night, throwing a wave over his shoulder to Suze, then he was reeling in the cool, damp air and the alcohol in his system began to dissipate.

"Sorry," he said, blurting that out first and foremost, before trying to gather his dizzy thoughts for something a bit more coherent. "He's not usually like that. I swear, he's not some" — he glanced around, uncertain if it was wise to spell it out — "judgemental bigot."

Gabriel was rummaging in his pockets, his face tense under the glow of a streetlamp.

"He's just being a drunk twat," Aled finished weakly and Gabriel shrugged.

"S'fine," he said.

"You're upset."

"Well, yeah, a stranger just said having a vagina makes me a girl despite the rather obvious fact I haven't shaved in two weeks and I've got more of a beard than he does," Gabriel returned waspishly, then lit up a cigarette and took a long drag. "Want one?"

"Don't smoke. You — okay?"

"Mm. You get used to it. Just doesn't happen as much anymore."

"Why?"

"Because people don't know," Gabriel said, snorting. "Five years ago, I looked female. People came out with that bollocks all the time. And the kind of people who do, don't generally want to fuck you on Grindr, so they don't come over. Getting it to my face...I'm out of practice, I guess."

Aled hesitated, then slid an arm around Gabriel's waist and kissed the cold leather of the jacket at his shoulder. "Suze'll kill him for you."

Gabriel scrunched his shoulder to his neck and pulled a face. "It's not *that* bad, really — like you said, he was drunk."

"Still shouldn't have said it. She'll rip him a new one. And if he sees you again, he'll be falling over himself to apologise."

Gabriel cracked a smile at that and ducked his head under Aled's to allow a bit of a cuddle. Aled pressed the advantage, nosing at Gabriel's now-damp hair.

"Come home with me?" he bargained. "We could be quick and get a taxi. I'll pay. And I'll take you to bed and do whatever you want to any body part you want."

Gabriel laughed, pulling away and holding out the burning cigarette as if to ward Aled off. "In the state you're in, you'll offer a clumsy handjob and fall asleep halfway through."

"Nope," Aled said, even though the pavement was dipping underneath him and he felt more than a bit sick. "Promise. Vanilla on the sofa, or I could tie you to the bed, or whatever you want. Except a beating, I'm too drunk to beat you."

"You're barely sober enough to beat me *off*," Gabriel retorted tartly, but then he smiled and stubbed the fag end out on the brickwork of the pub. "All right, my knight in shining winklepickers. Rescue me from the office girls, take me home and deflower me on your stairs."

Aled ducked in for a kiss, was denied then found himself being dragged towards the train station—or, presumably, the taxi rank outside it.

"Does this mean I have to get you flowers?" he asked.

* * * *

They ended up getting a taxi home. It cost a fortune and Gabriel was weirdly hands-off all the way home and it wasn't until Aled stumbled out of the cab and stared at his own garage door that he twigged.

"Fuck," he said. "I stink of booze, don't I?"

Gabriel laughed. "A little bit."

"That's why you won't touch me."

"Well, yeah."

"Right," Aled said, stabbing the key at the door and missing entirely, scraping the frame. "Shit. Right. I'll go—sober up, um, wash—fuck, what even—"

Gabriel made a faintly amused noise and took the keys away, unlocking the door as though he lived there. "You have a shower, brush your teeth and gargle some mouthwash. I will make some coffee or something. Then, when you don't taste and smell of something that makes me crazy in a bad way, you can make me crazy in a good way."

"Like how?" Aled asked, grinning and snagging his fingers into the waistband of Gabriel's jeans.

"Like whatever you can think of that'll have me begging you to do it more," Gabriel murmured, his breath washing over Aled's ear, then he bit the earlobe—and pushed Aled away. "Shower first."

Aled grinned, staggering upstairs. Despite the invitation, though, he took his time—both to ensure that the smell would be gone, but also to try to sober up a little, turning the temperature right down to try shocking the booze out of his system. Afterwards, he was generous with the deodorant, and even more so with the toothpaste and mouthwash, until his gums were stinging from the rough treatment.

Then, and only then, did he dare leave the bathroom. Full of intent, he left himself only in his towel, stealing back downstairs otherwise naked.

Only to find that the house was silent.

For a split second, Aled thought Gabriel had gone again, but then a light flickered outside and he ducked into the conservatory to open the door and squint at the cigarette glowing by the gate.

"All right?"

"Mm."

"So, you're fully dressed and smoking in my back garden, while I'm here naked in a towel—"

"Naked?" That got some attention and Gabriel stepped back into the light pooling on the patio from the open door. He grinned, eyeing Aled from head to toe. "Give me two minutes with this."

"Make it ten seconds," Aled said and started to massage his dick through the towel. "I've sobered up plenty and my cock knows it."

"Yeah? And what does your cock want?"

"It wants anything involving you. It's not fussy tonight."

"Yeah?" Gabriel stubbed out the cigarette and tossed the butt over the fence. Aled rolled his eyes, but drew Gabriel back into the conservatory by the neck of his T-shirt, and kissed him.

"Better?" he breathed when he let go again and Gabriel blinked slowly, eyes blown dark and hazy.

"Better," he murmured and nudged closer for a second. His stubble rasped harshly on Aled's skin and he tasted of smoke and ash. Aled didn't much care. He dropped his towel, seized Gabriel's arse in both hands and ground against the front of his jeans until Gabriel broke the kiss to bury his lips in Aled's neck and whine.

"I want those thighs wrapped around my head and I want to tongue-fuck you until you can't breathe," Aled growled.

"You gonna suck me off while you're down there?"

"Naturally."

"Then I think maybe you could get what you want."

"Good, drop your trousers."

Gabriel laughed at the blunt tone and Aled slapped his arse. "Hey!"

"I wasn't kidding. Drop them. You can drop them in the next thirty seconds or I can rip them off you and gag you with your own belt."

"I'm not just dropping my jeans here and letting you eat me out on the conservatory floor. Shower? I want to freshen up first."

Aled sighed. "Okay, but just the bar soap. I want to taste *you*, not my Radox."

"You use *Radox*? God, you sure *you* weren't the one born with a set of ovaries?"

Aled slapped his arse again and Gabriel fled up the stairs, laughing. Aled shook his head, palming his half-hard cock, before following, locking up the house along the way. Gabriel had left a clothes trail, his leather jacket at the bottom of the stairs and his underwear just outside the bathroom door, and Aled dutifully collected them all. By the time he heard the water shut off, Aled had even managed a quick one off the wrist to take the edge off. Eating out properly required concentration, after all.

He stole into the bathroom once the water had stopped running and caught Gabriel at the sink, cosying up to his back and kissing his neck. Gabriel had put his boob-flattening vest back on, but his only other defence was a towel and Aled casually undid the knot and let it fall. That incredible arse was left on full display and Aled kissed his way down Gabriel's spine, slowly sinking to his knees as his mouth tracked lower, and buried his teeth in one perfect cheek. Gabriel gasped, stilling in his grip for a moment, then began to squirm and pull away.

"*Don't*," he pleaded, twisting away when Aled tried to catch him. "That's *torture*, I can't grind one out on my feet. Take me to at least a warm floor before you start *biting*, God."

Aled surged to his feet, seizing Gabriel around the chest from behind and biting his shoulder through the thin cotton of the vest.

"Better run," he breathed as he released his jaw. "If I catch you before you reach the bed, I'll do you on the carpet and you'll have rug burn for weeks."

Then he let go and Gabriel bolted. Aled grinned, glad for the preparatory wank. He opened the bathroom cabinet to find his favoured lubricant for taste — less for actual lubrication, more for Aled's firm belief that the messier the better when it came to oral — and followed at a leisurely pace.

Gabriel had a middle-of-the-bed thing, having piled up the pillows behind him in the dead centre, and was already waiting with his legs spread and his knees bent, propped up just enough to watch, and rubbing himself in idle circles. "Away with those," Aled said, batting his hands aside as he settled behind Gabriel's knees. "If you need to touch something, you have nipples."

"They don't work."

"Then find something else that does." He smoothed his fingers over dry, hot skin at Gabriel's hips and thighs first, picking out little flaws in the alabaster and biting them — a mole below his bellybutton, stretch marks, thin and silvery, on his inner thigh, a tiny scar creating a groove by his hip-bone, ancient and alluring. Only after the bites did he begin to play, spreading the lube generously over his fingers and smearing it over Gabriel's thighs and cock, licking it away in broad strokes before replacing it, until Gabriel's fingers began to play with his hair in half-impatient, half-encouraging tugs.

Once the scent of synthetic strawberry filled his nose, Aled chased the reality and probed with his tongue, seeking out Gabriel's natural taste under slick oil and a lingering bland soap. He took his time, spreading his fingers across Gabriel's stomach and hips when he explored, gripping handfuls of his arse when he bit at those sensitive inner thighs. When Gabriel tired and locked his knees around the back of Aled's neck, he tracked lower still to give the promised tongue-fuck, smoothing lube into Gabriel's swollen dick in hard presses and soft swipes designed to tease, to torture, but not to bring him to a completion.

It did, though, eventually — Gabriel's incoherent whispering turned into a sharp panting and his thighs tightened. Aled gripped his hips in both hands, wrapping his lips around the hood of Gabriel's cock and sucking until he screamed, and pinned him as he came, massaging the shaking flesh between his teeth with a ghost of a threat behind it.

And when Gabriel relaxed again, shuddering and whining, Aled only sucked harder.

"Oh God —"

"I can do this for hours, sweetheart," Aled breathed, tugging on the thin skin separating Gabriel's thigh from his sex with his teeth, until Gabriel began to breathlessly cry above him. "Shall we see how often I can get you off before my dick gets jealous of my tongue and wants to have a turn?"

"Oh my God, yes, please."

Aled grinned, then returned to nuzzle his face against burning skin and lick Gabriel clean with a single-minded focus.

After all, there was only a third of the lube bottle left. And Aled hated to waste it.

Chapter Twenty

It had been a shit day.

From the pouring rain and the non-existent bus on his way to work, to the guy who recognised him from Grindr and called him a tranny faggot at the top of his lungs, thus outing him to the entire shop, it hadn't been one of Gabriel's finer Fridays. And when the lad at the next till had screwed up his face and said, "So you're a bird who's a bit fucked in the head, then?" Gabriel had just walked out.

Just taken off his name tag, put on his jacket and left.

He'd be sacked. He could see it coming. His boss was a tool and would sack him just for finding out he was trans, never mind actually breaking the rules and ditching a shift halfway through.

Then just as he reached Lidl, the nail in the coffin.

notyouraveragegaymer: sorry but I don't do slags pretending to be dudes to get more cock. You're just a slut with a short haircut :/

He got that kind of message all the time. He usually just rolled his eyes and deleted them. But — but —

Just today, just this once, it was too much. Something cracked inside his chest. His vision blurred. He had to swipe angrily at his face to stop the tears spilling over before he went straight for the retail therapy, marching into the KFC next door and ordering enough chicken to feed a small town. And when the thought crossed his mind that it would be so easy to just wander into the booze aisle at Lidl, Gabriel turned his back on everything and ran home — through the pouring rain, past the same bus that would take him two-thirds of the way there — to forget about his bloody awful day. To wallow until it stopped hurting, then return to jerking off to the memory of Aled using a whole bottle of lube to eat him out, or Kevin fucking him blind in that swing, or even Michael fucking him up against the front door like he couldn't wait another second.

Only the memories felt sour and ugly.

Sex.

That was all he was good for, right?

Just sex.

So when Michael texted, *Buy you dinner if you put those pretty lips around my dick for dessert?* it made Gabriel feel ill.

And when Aled texted, *Free tonight? Got a game here that I think you'd enjoy*, it made him feel even worse.

God, what was so wrong about enjoying sex? Why was it so much *worse* if he was trans? Trans women were all hookers and whores, and trans men were neutered, sexless *things*. Why was he such a *freak* if he liked sex? Lots of guys liked sex! Why was it suddenly so whorish and disgusting if *he* did? He was on a hook-up site for *sex*, for fuck's sake—what did *notyouraveragegaymer* think anybody else was there for?

But then, nobody else was Gabriel.

Nobody else was a slag pretending to be a dude to get more cock.

Nobody else was a slut with a short haircut.

Because he wasn't a *real* man. Because he wasn't *born* one. Because *his* breasts weren't weight-related. Because *his* dick was only two inches long and *his* testosterone came in a vial.

Because *bullshit.*

A few tears began to brim over and Gabriel swallowed scratchily, scrubbing at his eyes before thumbing out a shaky, *Sorry not feeling well* to both Michael and Aled, and chucking the phone onto the coffee table. God, he needed a good cry. And to curl up with the fleece blankets, and watch crap TV, and maybe later—when he felt a bit less shit—he could go job-hunting online and find somewhere else to work, where his colleagues didn't act like he was disgusting and his customers didn't scream abuse in his face.

So for a while, that was exactly what Gabriel did. He changed into his almost-never-worn pyjamas, huddled up on the sofa under his collection of fluffy blankets, stared at TV re-runs without really watching and turned over his shit job and his shit day in his head like they were on repeat. Maybe he dozed. Maybe he didn't. Either way, he stopped thinking for a while, and after a time, the tears dried up and just left him feeling congested and crap instead. The phone beeped several times and he ignored it. The neighbours upstairs started arguing and he ignored them. He ignored everything but his own shredded feelings and fully intended to do so for the rest of the night.

Until someone started knocking on the door.

Gabriel groaned and pulled the blankets over his head, not wanting to face the Mormons, or the traveller kids selling stolen crap or the bailiffs asking where next door were. He just wanted to be left alone.

But his visitor had other ideas — the knocking turned to banging, turned to hammering, turned to his *phone* starting to ring on the coffee table, then —

"Gabe! I can *hear* you're home! If you don't answer me, I'm going to have someone kick this door down!"

Gabriel blinked stupidly at the TV for a minute. Aled? Why the hell was Aled —

The phone stopped ringing and the end of Aled's demand caught up to him. "Shit!" He lurched up out of his blanket nest in a sudden panic — he couldn't afford to have the door put back on its hinges after some big-booted copper took it off them — and lunged for the security chain. "Hang on!" he called, wrestling with it, then finally managed to haul back the bolt and open the door.

Only for a hand to land squarely on his forehead and Aled to frown.

"Christ," he said. "You all right?"

"I'm — yeah, sorry, what are you doing here?"

Aled stared, then suddenly went red and coughed. He shuffled his feet and Gabriel glanced down to see a bag of shopping.

"Did you bring me food?"

"Amongst other things," Aled said. "I've been texting you all afternoon to see if you felt better and when you didn't answer, I — I got worried. So I thought I'd come and check."

A lump caught in Gabriel's throat and his lip wobbled alarmingly. Aled's embarrassed expression turned swiftly to alarm, and the dam broke, and Gabriel felt his own tear ducts betray him.

"Oh, *hell*, sweetheart, what's wrong?"

The endearment was even worse. Then Gabriel was being hugged, his face pressed into the cold shoulder of Aled's coat, and he clung even as he berated himself for the crack. God, how *pathetic*. Aled had just come over because someone he fucked and played pool with that one time wasn't feeling well, and Gabriel had to *cry* about it?

"Hey, hey, hey, come on, it's all right—"

"I just had a fucking shit day at work and I was making an excuse so I could be a loser and hide in my blankets and watch shit TV and feel sorry for myself then you came over and you're being so fucking *nice*—"

"Because I *care*, you little psychopath," Aled chided, his voice gentle despite the words. Gabriel choked, then forced himself away enough to bury his face in his hands and try to hide the meltdown. "Oh, hell. Hey. *Hey.* It's all right—"

"It's *not*, this is so fucking pathetic, I'm not supposed to go to fucking pieces just because someone cares, it's not like you're the only person who's ever worried about me, or—"

Aled's hands gripped his wrists tightly and Gabriel was forced to drop them with a gasp at the flare of pain. Then Aled's eyes were very close and very intent.

"*Breathe.*"

Startled, and held by the gaze, Gabriel found himself inhaling almost automatically at the command.

"And out again."

He exhaled.

"Good." Aled's voice had dropped into a low, commanding rumble. "In. And out." Gabriel obeyed. "What were you doing when I arrived?"

"I — um — sofa."

Aled glanced past him and a smile creased that freckled face. "All right. Back to the sofa with you. I'm going to put away this lot, then I'll come and join you. Without panic attacks. Okay?"

"Okay," Gabriel whispered.

He felt wrung-out and oddly thin, his fingers shaking slightly, and he dropped to the sofa with a groan as Aled made himself thoroughly at home in Gabriel's kitchenette. He felt hotly embarrassed — but also fragile, like Aled had taken a hammer and smashed him in his glass jaw with it. Cracked, but not shattered.

"Hey," Aled said softly when he was done, coming to perch on the coffee table and peer at Gabriel's face, ducking down so that his eyes looked huge. "What do you need?"

Gabriel opened his mouth — and hesitated. A hug. Love. Someone to tell him he wasn't a freak. Someone to rant about his colleagues. Someone to *punch* his colleagues. Sex. To be stripped off and thought of as gorgeous and fuckable. To be held.

"Hug," he croaked eventually, deciding that left the least cracks on show. Then he was warm, Aled's arms closing like a trap around him, and a kiss landing on the side of his head.

"Can I guess," Aled murmured, rocking them slightly, "that is a feelings type of ill rather than a bug or an injury type of ill?"

"Yeah."

"Feels-ill."

Gabriel started. *"Feels?* What?"

"Oh, shut up," Aled grumbled, then untangled himself and started to settle on the sofa with Gabriel instead of hugging him over a coffee table. He sat back against the arm and tugged Gabriel to lie between his legs and rest over his chest. Gabriel steadily rebuilt the nest of blankets around them, as Aled tried to work out how to use his remote control. When he found some documentary, his arms came back around Gabriel's shoulders and his lips found their way to Gabriel's scalp.

"You want to talk about it?"

"No," Gabriel mumbled.

"Okay. I'll hug it out."

Gabriel smiled faintly and buried his nose in Aled's shirt. He felt jagged and wanted to cry some more, but the testosterone made it oddly difficult to cry sometimes. His eyes stayed itchy and dry, and he slowly relaxed under the stroking motion of Aled's hand up and down his back.

"Sorry for being a basket case," he mumbled.

Aled's chest rose jerkily in a chuckle and he traced the shell of Gabriel's ear. "S'fine," he said. "I just wanted to check you weren't passed out in your shower."

"Passing out on you is better?"

"Much better. It counts as a cuddle."

"Octopus," Gabriel said half-heartedly, wanting to go back to the weekend, and the all-consuming fuck on Aled's sofa, and toad-in-the-hole. Wanting to go back to just being happy and nobody giving him shit for being *him*.

His chest tightened and Aled squeezed the back of his neck lightly.

"Just relax, sweetheart. I've got a medical degree in hugging out feels-ill. Just trust me."

Gabriel laughed, a little too thinly, and curled his hand into Aled's T-shirt, bunching up the heat and the smell in a fist, then slowly, deliberately, releasing every finger one by one.

He didn't remember getting to the last one.

* * * *

Gabriel woke up to someone handling his feet.

So he kicked.

"Fuck!"

Then his brain restarted and he grimaced. "Oh, God, I'm so sorry—"

"Christ, you scared the shit out of me," Aled complained, picking himself up from his spectacular crash-landing off the end of the sofa.

"I just—"

Aled's face softened and he stooped to kiss Gabriel's hand and prise it away from his face to find his mouth. "It's fine, you missed my face," he said and pressed a kiss to Gabriel's mouth. "I made curry. You want some?"

Gabriel's stomach voiced its approval and Gabriel nodded, scrubbing the sleep out of his face and curling his feet up towards his body, where they couldn't randomly kick people.

"You want a lot, or are you one of those people who doesn't want to eat when they're upset?"

"No, I eat my own body weight in crap when I'm upset."

"Just as well, I kind of overdid it…"

Gabriel was soon presented with a ridiculously large bowl of rogan josh, complete with rice and warm naan bread, and tucked his feet back into Aled's lap when beckoned to do so. Aled resumed the massage, digging his thumbs into the arch until Gabriel wanted to dissolve and rubbing between his toes in tiny sweeps and digs.

"Mind if I stay the night?"

Gabriel shrugged and Aled rapped the top of his foot. "Ow!"

"Do you want me to stay the night or not?"

"I — fine, yes, I would like that, but it won't be any fun for you."

"Apart from the bit where you burst into tears when I said I cared, it's been plenty fun," Aled scolded in a mild tone, then tugged on Gabriel's ankle. "Actually, I might have had an epiphany."

"About what?"

"When I go home — tonight or tomorrow, whenever — I'm getting divorced."

Gabriel nearly dropped his spoon. "Um, what?"

"I'm going to sign the papers."

"You — but you were so — "

"I've been so far in denial, I nearly hit Sudan."

"What?"

Aled rolled his eyes. "The Nile?"

"Isn't that in Egypt?"

"And Sudan, farther upriver. Not the point," he added. "The point is, both you and Suze saw I was moving on, but I didn't. I didn't want to admit it."

"Why?"

Aled paused, the interruption throwing him. "I — suppose because marriage means something to me. I don't expect you'd understand that."

"No," Gabriel replied frankly.

"Well, it does. To me. And I got married to prove to the world how much I loved my wife and I did it *when*

I did it to ensure my father could see me married before he died. I feel like I failed because it broke down—but I think I've come to terms with it being over, even if I still don't like the fact."

"How do you know?"

"You."

Gabriel blinked, eyes wide and dark over the bowl.

"We weren't monogamous, me and Melissa. We both slept with other people—with consent. She liked certain scenes that I couldn't do for her and I just took it as an equal agreement. If she was allowed to play away, then so was I, so sometimes I did. But I'm not—I can sleep with anyone if I like their body, but I can't fall in love when I already love someone else. I've never been able to do it. I can't imagine being able to do it. I don't understand how poly relationships would work on that level, because for me, it *wouldn't* work."

"I don't get it," Gabriel said slowly.

"I just took your bins out, Gabe."

" —riel!"

"I just made dinner and changed the sheets on your bed and did—housekeeping. Housework. While you were asleep. I didn't go home, I didn't wake you up for a bit of company or a bit of fun—Suze was right. I'm moving on and you're the one making me do it. I *forgot* about the divorce pack in my kitchen drawer. I *forgot* about sorting a solicitor to fend off Melissa's. You've got me *forgetting* about my divorce and doing housework in your flat just because you're not feeling right tonight."

Gabriel swallowed and started to chew on his lip. "Aled—"

Aled squeezed his foot and jostled it gently. "I'm not saying I want us to jump right into some exclusive partnership and you need to move in with me," he said softly. "I'm not even saying I want anything to change between us. I *like* us, like we are. I'm just saying, there's emotional stakes now. For me."

Gabriel licked his lips. "You're saying you think of me as your..."

"Boyfriend. Partner. Better half. Whatever you want to call it."

"I'm not—I'm not boyfriend material, Aled."

"Why?"

"I *do* fall in love with other people. I—"

"And I don't mind," Aled whispered earnestly. "I mean it—I might not be capable of it myself, but I don't mind if you do it, as long as you're honest with me. As long as you love me as well."

There was a pregnant pause. Gabriel flushed.

"I don't. Yet."

"Yet?"

"It's—I do...I love you, but I'm not in love with you. Yet."

Aled smiled. "A trust thing?"

Gabriel let out a shaky, relieved breath. "A bit, yeah."

"Maybe I can work on that, too," he said, stroking his fingertips over Gabriel's toes in soft sweeps. "Persuade and coax you into being in love with me, as well as trusting me."

Gabriel smiled faintly. "Maybe."

"I do want a relationship with you, Gabriel. A proper one. Dates. Silly days out. Trips away sometimes. Games. Spending more time together. But I'm not asking to be your only. Just...one of the higher priority guys."

Gabriel laughed and Aled grinned, rubbing at his skin like he was brushing off cobwebs.

"Is that a yes, let's try this out?"

"It's a, you're insane, getting divorced to try and pin down a poly guy."

Aled's smile faded and he eyed Gabriel's feet in his lap, tracing their veins with the nail of his pinky finger.

"I...don't think I am," he said softly. "I think it's like what Suze said. I love Melissa. I'm always going to love her, even if I'm not *in* love with her anymore. And if I love her, I have to let her go. Like I wouldn't try and keep a hold of you if you wanted out. Like I won't try and demand exclusivity from you when you're not wired that way. I wouldn't do it to you, so why am I doing it to her?"

"Because it's harder to let go than it is to never take hold in the first place," Gabriel said quietly.

"Maybe."

Gabriel shifted, placing the bowl on the side, then crawled up the sofa to wriggle into Aled's lap, looping his arms around Aled's neck.

"I don't belong to you," he said clearly, "and I am never going to be *just* yours. I'll play with other guys. I might just fuck them, I might love them. I have other regulars. You don't get a say in how that works, or what I do with them. But — if you can handle that, I'd like a bit more of you, too. I do like you. I do love you, to a certain extent. And I *want* to feel more for you. I want to be less wary and I want to find out what you're like in your *really* dominant moods. I want to play games with you, but — I want this, too. And maybe one day, I'd like to tolerate having to be hugged to death in my sleep every night, or your odd socks in my laundry, but I don't know if that could ever happen."

Aled ran his hands down Gabriel's back, firm and smooth. "Nobody ever knows that," he said. "So — is that an agreement? We're dating? I get to take you out to dinner and stake a claim on your birthday as being with me and not your other guys?"

"That would be *your* birthday. I spend *my* birthday with whoever the fuck I please," Gabriel retorted haughtily, then laughed and bumped his lips against Aled's for a sloppy kiss. "Okay. I *suppose* I can allow you to stake a *bit* of a claim. But only a bit of one."

"Fine by me," Aled said, nudging his nose against Gabriel's and grinning. "Want to get the rest of that curry down *then* we have a celebratory shag, or reheat it in the microwave *after* the celebratory shag?"

"Shag," Gabriel said, locking his thighs around Aled's hips and smiling against his cheekbone. "But you have to untangle me first."

Aled laughed and tumbled them down into the sofa, seizing at the waistband of Gabriel's jeans and ripping them open.

"Oh, I can do that."

Chapter Twenty-One

Aled took Gabriel home that night.

And he was still there when Aled got home on Thursday evening. He'd made a fairly decent fish pie, and Aled subjected him to more of the SyFy channel, and he was woken up at four in the morning by Gabriel sneaking back into bed after a trip to the bathroom.

The bad mood passed fairly quickly, but it left a mark on Aled's mind. He'd been allowed to see it. He'd genuinely thought it was physical until he'd seen Gabriel's face — the man was just so *cheerful* normally — but once it had passed and he was whining about the bad acting and prodding more pie down Aled's neck, Aled moved on to the real significance of the whole incident.

Gabriel had let him see it. Gabriel had let him stay. And Gabriel had followed him home and stayed a bit longer.

Aled made the mistake of telling Suze on Friday morning at work. She immediately booked a table at their favourite posh pub and said it was the perfect time for Tom to apologise for his crass comments on the bar crawl.

"Suze, I really don't think—"

"He needs to. So you'll both come, right? Right!"

Then she got the mutinous look on her face and Aled caved in. So he spent the rest of the day texting Gabriel—half of them warnings about Suze's plan and the other half trying not to get hard from a series of naked selfies. Every time Aled texted a negative mood—be it that he was bored, annoyed or even hungry—Gabriel would reply with a naked selfie and a caption. The reply to hungry was downright pornographic.

And slowly, a plan unfurled.

They'd never played the promised game they'd talked about. The hoodie didn't really count, in Aled's eyes. And with Gabriel being a merciless tease and Suze insisting on them all having dinner together this evening—

A plan formed, somewhere between the shower selfie and the food porn, and Aled knew exactly what game he wanted to start with.

Didn't help with the trying-to-work situation, though.

Thankfully, though, Suze left at two for an eye test and Aled was left in peace when Gabriel said he was going into town to fill his prescription. Over the last two hours of the shift, Aled—and his dick—were left to recover.

Until a minute to five, when Gabriel sent a selfie of himself with his head leaning against a car number plate. Ending RDF. *Aled's* car number plate.

Me: GET. OFF. THE CAR!

Gabriel Grindr: Not touching it!

Bollocks he wasn't.

Aled logged off. Screw being on time. He was going to take Gabriel home and beat him until his arse was red if he'd touched Aled's car. If it made them late for dinner, then so be it.

Only, when he stormed outside, it wasn't Gabriel who caught his attention.

"Aled!"

Shit.

"Melissa, I'm running late, I—"

She stormed over from her car and slapped him in the chest with a handful of papers, and a pen. "Sign them."

"Melissa—"

"Sign them!"

"I'll—I'll have a look…"

"No!" Her eyes were like fire. She looked breathtakingly beautiful and terrifyingly angry. Aled actually took a step back. "Stop fucking stalling and sign them!"

His own temper flickered into life. "I need to talk to a solicitor before I sign anyway!"

"So help me God, Aled, if you don't sign them this minute, I will take this to court! And if you make me take it to court, then I *will* take everything!"

"You've already taken everything!"

"I will take your house, I will take that damn car, I will take your money! If you make us go to court with this, I will make it the worst divorce you could possibly fucking imagine!" she raged. "So you can either sign the damn papers and stop fucking us both over, or I can take us to court, fuck *you* over and you'll have to sign them anyway!"

"You're not the only person in this fucking marriage, Melissa!" he bellowed, losing the precarious hold he had on his emotions. "You've drawn up these papers without a word to me about it, thrown them at me without giving us the chance to work it out and you're mad I'm not just fucking signing them without even having a lawyer look over them first!"

"If you loved me, you'd sign them!"

Aled seized the papers from her hands and tore them into shreds. Then, for good measure, he turned and hurled the pen at the automatic doors. They didn't register it and its cheap plastic casing broke apart on the glass.

"I'm not fucking signing anything," he hissed through clenched teeth, "until a lawyer — *my* lawyer — goes through it. I have your other copies at home. I will get someone to look at them next week. Until then, back the fuck off."

"You've had time!"

"I need more! I only just got my head around us being over!" he bellowed. "I still love you and you walked out without a fucking word, after —"

"I had plenty of words! I was in *bits* after they diagnosed you and you didn't give a shit!"

"*Diagnosed* me? For fuck's sake, Melissa, it's not terminal bloody cancer!"

"That would have hurt less!"

It echoed around the car park and brought Aled up short. His mind reeled. Terminal *cancer* would have — have hurt less? Was she serious? She'd rather he'd had terminal cancer, than —

"Er."

Melissa turned on the new voice, apoplectic, and shouted, "What!" in a wide-eyed Gabriel's face.

"Whoa, relax—"

"Who the fuck are you? Aled! Who the fuck is he? He's been at your car—oh my God. Have you been harping on at me for moving on, when you've been shag—"

"Urgh, Christ, no thanks, missus!"

Aled blinked, Gabriel's suddenly coarse voice cutting across the fog in his brain. It had deepened into a sharp chirp, twanging strangely over the vowels. It sounded almost Cockney, deeply southern, not blurred with the Yorkshire twang he'd picked up in the north. It wasn't Leeds. It wasn't even *Gabriel*.

"Not exactly my type, mate. I'm just hitching a lift. But you two wanna get your lawyers sorting it out instead of bawling in public? S'just, you know, I reckon Huddersfield might not have caught the last bit."

Melissa pursed her lips and turned on her heel. She marched back to her car, shouting over her shoulder. "My solicitor will be in touch. And if *yours* doesn't reply within the week, Aled, I'll take you to court and take *everything*."

Aled simply stared, until her car door slammed and the engine revved. Then, slowly, he stepped out of the pile of paper shards at his feet and swallowed.

"You okay?" Gabriel said softly.

"She said cancer would have hurt less," Aled whispered numbly.

Gabriel bit his lip. "Hey. Maybe dinner's not a good idea—"

Aled shook himself. As Melissa's car disappeared into the tea-time traffic, Gabriel came closer and rubbed a hand up Aled's arm, squeezing his elbow briefly.

"What do you need?" he whispered.

Aled shook his head. "To not think about what she just said."

"Well, think about this, then," Gabriel said, fumbling with his phone, then showed Aled a selfie of himself, clearly leaning his back against Aled's windscreen.

"Fucker," Aled croaked, then swallowed and scrubbed a hand across his eyes. "No, we're going to dinner. I just need to—re-group a bit."

"Tell you what," Gabriel said. "Your place. Bend me over the side of the sofa and beat my arse raw for sitting on your car. Then come in my mouth to put me back in my place. Then we can have a quick shower and go out for *massive* burgers with your friends to make up for the lost energy. Yeah?"

Aled rallied himself, nodding. "Yeah. And, um. Thanks. For heading her off. Even though that blokey act was faintly disturbing."

Gabriel smirked. "Just because I'm a flirty, fuckable queer doesn't mean I don't know how to be the builder's apprentice next door, you know."

"You certainly know how to fuck him," Aled mumbled, then squared his shoulders. "Right. Car. Let's go. And you can sit in the back seat, take your jeans off and get your arse ready for me later. Because I won't be gentle."

* * * *

Aled pulled his softened, spent cock out and slapped Gabriel's abused arse. A mix of lube and cum was beginning to escape and Aled opened the bathroom cabinet to find a suitable plug.

"You won't be putting that arse on my car again," he said casually, leaning over the bath to present the chosen plug to Gabriel's mouth. "Suck on it."

Gabriel was bent over the side of the bath, bracing himself by his hands on the tiles opposite. The shower was raining down on him, freezing cold and causing him to splutter and cough all the way through what had been a brutal fuck. And yet apparently Gabriel was a glutton for punishment, for he turned his face away from the plug and refused.

"Fine. But if it comes out, I'll put it back. And fuck you again while it's still inside."

Gabriel choked as Aled shoved the plug in, burying it to the base, and twisted it until Gabriel began to thrust back against him.

Because Gabriel hadn't—yet—come.

"You want me to touch you?"

"Please." His voice was ragged and breathless.

"You want to touch yourself?"

"Please."

"Tough," Aled said and slapped again. He left a handprint behind. Smirking, he fetched another plug from the cabinet. "You're leaking from both sides. I'll not be having that mess all over my house and car."

Gabriel whined when the second plug was inserted, and Aled smacked him.

"Quiet. And stay there. If you move an inch, I'll chain you to the taps and give you an ice bath. Got it?"

"Y-yes, sir."

The unexpected honorific made blood pool in Aled's groin again, but it was too soon. He flicked the base of one plug before leaving the bathroom, rummaging in his bedroom drawers for what he wanted, before returning. Gabriel was built like Melissa. Slim hips, small arse. So —

"You wanted to play a game, right?"

"Y-yes —"

"So, let's play."

Lo and behold, the chastity belt fit like a charm and Aled locked it into place. Gabriel seemed to realise what it was halfway through and twisted violently, so Aled seized him by the hair and shook him.

"Fuck me around and I'll leave it on for a week."

Gabriel stilled, gasping. Aled knew it would be torture. The plugs were bad enough, but the belt — a full around-the-waist style, that visually resembled little more than a pair of grey knickers — had been modified. Right now, a ring was rubbing up against Gabriel's cock, and it would tease him with every single step that he took.

And Gabriel, without the keys to the locks, would not be able to remove it.

"If you're good during dinner," Aled said, sliding the keys into his pocket and dragging Gabriel up from the bath by the shoulders, "then I'll take it off after dinner and let you come. If not" — he rubbed his thumb along Gabriel's bottom lip — "then it stays on."

"Yellow."

Aled paused, eyes searching Gabriel's face. Slowly, Gabriel shook his head.

"It comes off after dinner," he whispered.

Aled nodded and kissed that bottom lip. "Okay. Colour?"

"Green."

Aled nuzzled his cheek, then shoved him roughly towards the door. "Get dressed. I need a shower. Be ready by the front door when I'm done."

Gabriel disappeared and Aled turned up the heat on the still-running shower before stepping into it. He rolled his shoulders and sighed. The tension had leaked out of him with every thrust. And God, Gabriel had been incredible—protesting the whole way, but not fighting, refusing with closed lips and twisting motions, but not arguing. He'd played the barely broken-in submissive to perfection, acted the unwilling victim to Aled's desires like they'd been playing for years, and Aled intended to thoroughly reward him for it at some point. Either by any game Gabriel wanted, or just by taking him out for dinner and a movie sometime. Or both, if Gabriel was at incredible after the meal as he'd been before it.

Aled tipped his head back under the water, the heat massaging his shoulders and pushing away everything but the post-fuck feeling, and smiled.

Dinner was going to be…interesting.

Chapter Twenty-Two

Gabriel had never hated being driven anywhere so much in his entire life.

The plug was bad. But the chastity belt was worse. Not only was the very *existence* of such a device an affront to Gabriel's sex life, but that it was *on him* felt insulting. And yet its upgrade—namely that damned ring—was both an amazing sensation every time he moved, and a cruel reminder that no matter how much he wanted to, he couldn't just get a hand down his jeans and solve the problem.

"Fuck," he said conversationally, as Aled turned the car neatly into a parking space outside a country pub. "You."

Aled laughed. "You can safeword any time, you know."

Yes, he could. But he didn't want to, not really. Because if he did, it *would* stop the torture and it *would* let him be comfortable again. But it would also remove any chance Gabriel had of getting fucked blind in compensation for this later and he wasn't—quite—

willing to give that up. Especially after being bent over the bath earlier and fucked until it hurt. *Really* hurt. Which Aled hadn't done thus far and Gabriel didn't realise until he had how much it had been missing. No, Gabriel wanted his reward for this.

Didn't mean he couldn't let his displeasure be known, though, and he scowled when Aled pinched his thigh.

"Both of them know I'm into bondage and the like," he said quietly, "and Suze knows that I've started playing with you. But if *neither* of them guess you're being played with tonight, then I'll let you out of the belt and do whatever you want in the car."

"Fuck me dry."

Aled blinked. "There was already a bit of blood —"

"After this," Gabriel said, "it needs to hurt if you're even going to *begin* to take the edge off."

"Front door only."

"Okay. But dry."

Aled stared at him, then slowly nodded. "All right. Deal. I'll fuck you dry *if* neither of them guess I'm playing with you right now."

Gabriel grinned and Aled's expression hardened. Suddenly, he was gripping Gabriel's jaw in one hand and his face was much closer.

"You going to behave yourself?"

Gabriel's breath caught at the hot, hostile stare. "Yes, sir," he whispered, his tongue heavy and unwieldy in his mouth.

"You going to show me up in public?"

"No, sir."

"Fuck me around," Aled whispered, "and I'll strip you of everything, including that belt, tie you down to your own bed, and leave you there for a week. No sex. No contact. *Nothing.* Got it?"

Gabriel's heart skipped a beat. "I—got it. Got it."

"Behave yourself, and I'll take the belt off and fuck you in the back seat."

His heart outright staggered then, blood pooling in his groin, and he bit his lip to hide the moan. Aled's grip tightened on his jaw.

"Understood?"

"Yes, sir. I'll behave."

"Good. Get out."

The minute Aled let go, Gabriel schooled his expression and let himself out. He'd grown up gay in a homophobic, transphobic household. He was a *pro* at pretending to be something he wasn't, and right now, a dry fuck in a flash car was at stake. He would be a picture of saintly composure.

The pub was the fancy type with a restaurant, rather than a normal one with bar food, and Aled's friends were already seated with pints of Stella. A waitress swooped in to catch them before they'd even sat down, and—despite the aggravation in his jeans—Gabriel was suitably distracted by the almost posh atmosphere. Aled called for two soft drinks, to Gabriel's surprise, before his attention was stolen by the hand thrust out to shake his.

"Sorry," said the bloke.

"Um—"

"I was a drunk dickhead last time we met," he continued blandly, "and I was bang out of order. I was curious, but I don't know you and I was being inappropriate. So, I'm sorry. Start over?"

Gabriel stared. For a split second, he didn't know what to say. Nobody had ever actually apologised to him for being a dick before. People tended to get defensive and insist it wasn't rude or inappropriate and say he was being too sensitive. So he wasn't really sure what to *do* with an apology.

"Er—that's all right," he said slowly and shook the still-outstretched hand.

"It's not really," the bloke said, pulling a face. "Always would have said I was supportive of gay folks and everything but coming out with what I did wasn't. But I am sorry and it won't happen again."

"Until the next time you get several pints down your neck," the woman—Suze, Gabriel remembered—added snidely, then turned a big smile on him. "Sit down and just let me know if this berk here needs another smack. I ripped him a new one for being a jerk already."

"Tom, wasn't it?"

He'd guessed right and slowly relaxed as Tom turned the conversation to dating apps and explaining how he'd gotten into trouble for that, too, once Suze had found out he was using a Grindr account. Tom, it transpired, was extremely straight. And Suze, his long-suffering girlfriend, was extremely sceptical.

"It's just a bit of fun," Tom insisted as the starters arrived. "Nobody uses Grindr to actually get a *date*."

"Aled did!" Suze said hotly.

"That was about sex!"

"No, it wasn't—that's how he met *Gabriel*!"

"And we met for sex," Gabriel interrupted calmly, trying—and failing—not to think about sex given the state of his...well, everything between his knees and his waist.

"You fucked my brother. Or he fucked you. Did—"

"*Tom!*"

"Aled did mention it," Gabriel said, smirking a little. He remembered Daz—a larger-than-life Cornishman with a mad grin and his tall-dark-and-handsome type of a boyfriend. They'd been a lot of fun. He still regretted not just having a threesome with them and being done with it. "I remember Daz. Huge —"

"Oh *God*!" Tom wailed.

" — personality."

"Right," Aled drawled. "Because you were interested in his *personality*."

"It was a great personality. With a cock like a sledgehammer to match," Gabriel added, enjoying watching Tom squirm and go purple with discomfort. Revenge, he decided. If Tom called him a girl again, Gabriel would just relive — or reinvent — Daz's abilities in bed. "I remember I hurt for a *week* after —"

"Now I know why you're shagging Aled. You're as bloody evil as he is," Tom whined and promptly — and very deliberately — changed the subject to some fantasy football league that he and Aled bought into. Which was beyond Gabriel's level of caring. Real football was bad enough. *Fantasy* was just sad.

Then he made the mistake of sitting back from his finished starter and stiffened as the ring slid tantalisingly down his skin.

Fuck.

His breath caught in his chest, sudden and sharp, and he felt Suze's watchful eye suddenly on him. "Gabriel?" Her voice sounded oddly echoey for a moment and he blinked. "Gabriel? Are you all right?"

"Fine," he said, seizing his composure. "Just — need a quick smoke. Before they bring the main. You know."

She narrowed her eyes. Aled didn't so much as twitch, rolling his eyes and making a snide comment about cancer sticks. Gabriel didn't care. He didn't pause, either, rummaging for his lighter and lurching gracelessly up from the table, banging his knee in the process. The burst of pain interrupted the rising fire in his blood and he managed to escape into the cold night air.

And breathe.

Breathe.

"Fuck," he whispered, leaning back against the wall. He spread his legs, desperate to alleviate the pressure. Fuck, this was going to kill him. *Aled* was going to kill him. By the time Gabriel *got* his fuck, he'd be crawling out of his own skin.

His fingers were trembling, and a sudden, vicious urge to have a drink seized him.

Instantly, his blood ran cold and he lit up.

"Stop it," he whispered to himself, drawing heavily on the cigarette. "Get it together. You don't need a fucking drink."

The smoke curled, silvery grey in the frosty air, and he inhaled a sharp, cold lungful of the night before returning the fag end to his lips.

"Light?"

He jumped. Tom, a shadow in the open doorway, smirked and held out a cigarette between his fingers.

"Shit, sorry, sure —"

The lighter flared between them and Tom smiled companionably. "All right?"

"Yeah."

"You look stressed."

"Pub," Gabriel lied shortly. "Don't go in them much."

"Drink problem?"

Gabriel gave him a look. Tom shrugged.

"Wouldn't be the only bloke I know."

"Dry now."

"Yeah?"

"Have been for years."

"Good for you. Problem, was it, or —"

"Full-blown alcoholism."

"Bit young for that, aren't you?"

"You're never too young," Gabriel said bitterly. He'd been the youngest at the dry house by about ten years, but not in the original rehab centre. There'd been *kids* in there. Sixteen-, seventeen-year-old girls who'd knife a man for a bottle of cheap paint-stripper vodka.

"True. Look. Away from Suze and Aled — we good?"

Gabriel eyed him in the gloom. Tom was, he decided, a rather typical guy. None too bright about these things and prone to opening his mouth only to insert his foot — but harmless. Meaningless. He didn't mean things the way they sounded.

"Yeah," he said. "We're good."

They finished smoking in a warm silence, then headed back inside.

* * * *

With desserts down and sitting back in silence to nurse his cold Coke and try to resist the urge to adjust himself — and thus undoubtedly make it worse — Gabriel started to relax. Without him moving, the belt couldn't aggravate him as much. And the less it rubbed in all the right places, the more he could take in what was in front of him, namely, someone close enough to be Aled's sister, who was sizing him up more like she was Aled's mother.

And frankly, Gabriel was beginning to see why Aled's wife might have had issues with the best friend.

Aled and Suze were *close*. Gabriel couldn't put his finger on it exactly, but there was a kind of familiarity between them that was a bit too much for friends. They smiled too much, watched too often, leaned into each other's spaces like siblings didn't and like lovers *did*. By contrast, Suze sat almost apart from her actual boyfriend, who talked to Gabriel as though their respective partners weren't even there.

A smile quirked the edge of Gabriel's lip. Maybe Aled wasn't as monogamous when it came to love as he made out.

So when Aled excused himself for the call of nature before the bill arrived, Gabriel leaned across to Suze and said, "So when did you and Aled stop being a thing?"

Suze groaned. Tom laughed.

"I keep telling you!"

"And I keep telling everyone!" she complained, then fixed Gabriel with a stare. She had blue eyes and their hold was firm. "We've never been a thing."

"Right."

"We haven't! *You're* his thing now."

"Don't call me a thing." Gabriel's voice tightened, the echoes of countless messages calling him an *it* rising in his mind. Then he shook it off and shrugged. "Anyway, we're not. We screw. There's a difference."

"You don't love him?"

"I don't know him."

"But you play games with him."

"Some games. Not all."

"Like what?"

"I don't want to know what!" Tom interrupted hotly and Suze flashed him a dirty look that made Gabriel smirk.

"He's a prude," she said scornfully. "So how can you play with him at all if you don't trust him?"

"I didn't say I don't trust him."

"You said you didn't know him."

"Don't need to know him to trust him."

"Really?"

Gabriel rolled his eyes. "When you've fucked as many men as I have, and you're transgender to go with it, you learn to recognise someone you can trust a mile away. I don't trust him enough for certain games yet, but I trust him enough for the basics."

"Which are…?"

"Seriously, can we stop talking about what Aled likes to do to other blokes in bed? *Please*?"

Suze sat back, pulling a face. "Fine. I'm just saying, it's weird. He'd normally have you in a chastity belt by now if you trusted him, but you don't know him enough to love him?"

Gabriel shrugged, smirking. His pulse was beating too hard and too hot in his crotch, but in the wake of Suze's words, it felt amusing more than annoying. "I fuck a lot, I love far less often. And chastity's *really* not my thing."

"What's not your thing?" Aled asked, reappearing. The waitress interrupted, taking her chance and zipping across with the bill, and a heated argument ensued between Tom, who wished to be traditional and pay for both himself and his girlfriend as the man in the relationship, and Suze, who promptly emasculated him on principle and insisted on paying for everyone.

"It was my idea to come to dinner and, Tom, if you don't shut up, I'll fucking pack you back off to St Ives!" she seethed in the end and Aled laughed quietly in Gabriel's ear.

"Time to go, I think," he said and nudged Gabriel to stand.

Tom merely wanted to shake hands and pull a face or two. Suze wanted a hug and Gabriel ground his teeth through it as she pressed right up against him to do it — and finally, *finally*, they were out into the night again and the car was a gleaming beacon, lonely at the end of the car park.

"So, did she completely scare the shit out of you?"

"No, she's nice. And Tom apologised. Twice."

"Good."

"Did I pass the vetting?"

Aled laughed. "You noticed?"

"That was like dinner with your future in-laws."

"Oh God, don't, you'll give her ideas —"

"I win."

Aled glanced quizzically at him as they reached the car.

"They didn't guess."

He grinned. "No, you're right —"

"And you totally had a thing with Suze."

"Nope." Aled's reply was casual and almost bored, like he'd heard it all before. "If I could be in love with her, I would be. Now, is that what you want to do with your victory — ask questions about Suze — or —"

"She asked if I trust you."

"Do you?"

"Not completely. Not yet."

"Fair en —"

"She also asked if I love you."

Aled paused. It was a cold night and Gabriel frowned at the response, tugging on the locked car door.

"Unfreeze, please?"

"Sorry." The indicators flashed and Gabriel let himself in, turning on the heaters immediately. "What did you say?"

"Said I didn't know you enough to love you, but it makes me wonder why she thinks I would."

Aled pulled a face. "She wants me to fall in love and — go through with my divorce. She thinks you're the ticket."

Gabriel frowned a little at the twist that statement elicited in his chest, then shrugged it off. "That'd be daft of you, divorce a wife to get with a guy who sleeps around."

"So did my wife. Some of us don't mind a bit of sleeping around, now can we stop talking about my divorce and Suze being a meddling cow, and talk about what you want me to do to you?"

Gabriel bit his lip, thinking. He watched Aled's face — calm, but with a trace of impatience lurking under the skin — and decided. "I want you to make me trust you."

"Sorry?"

"You choose what to do. But whatever it is, I have to trust you. Role play a rape scene, tie me up and gag me, choke me — whatever you want. But it has to be something that needs me to trust you."

For a long moment, there was silence.

Then slowly, Aled's thumb came up to brush over Gabriel's bottom lip — and he shook his head.

"No."

"No?" Gabriel echoed.

"You can't force trust. And me gagging you and fucking you so you *can't* stop me won't make you trust me. If you want me to make you trust me, then we just carry on the way we're going and time will do the job on its own."

Gabriel cocked his head.

"You can name something else if you want, but asking me to *make* you trust me is asking for trouble. And I don't want that."

"You said test you."

"Not by—" Gabriel saw the moment that Aled twigged. He blinked, frowned, blinked again, then huffed an exasperated laugh. "*That* was a test."

"Uh-huh."

"It was — inventive, I'll give you that."

"I'm not in this game because I like it boring."

Aled coughed a laugh and shook his head. "Christ, you're mental."

"Maybe."

"Definitely. So *without* the testing, what do you want? I find it hard to believe you don't want *any*thing—"

"Oh, I didn't say that."

Chapter Twenty-Three

Two weeks later, Aled tied Gabriel to his bed, gagged him with a pair of socks and fucked him like a living fleshlight. Then left him there to make lunch. Then came back upstairs and fucked him again.

Like a live-in sex slave. Like a thing to be used. Like an object.

And afterwards, they cuddled on the sofa and Gabriel made fun of yet another SyFy programme — albeit one that *was* actually bad, to his credit — and Aled woke up in the middle of night to cold feet sliding up the backs of his thighs, toes wiggling against his leg hair to get warm.

It was —

Trust. And sex. Fun. And *something*.

He wasn't single anymore.

He wasn't exactly sure what he *was*, either. But he didn't keep booze in the house anymore. He had an extra key, hanging on the ring between his garage key and his house key. He went to a nightclub for the first time in years and kept a proprietary hand in Gabriel's back pocket. Sometimes he came home to someone cooking in his kitchen. Sometimes he left work and took the main road straight out to Belle Isle.

Things…were different.

One message on a hookup app had changed everything. His mood. His lack of energy. His wallowing. Gabriel had shaken the dust off, and sure, it was mostly sex. It had started with *just* sex. And more often than not, if Aled went over, they fucked. If Gabriel stayed the night, they fucked.

But sometimes they didn't.

And sometimes…

He'd never say it front of Gabriel, largely because he'd be mercilessly mocked for all eternity, but sometimes Aled was sure that they made love, as well as fucked. Sometimes, he caught himself wondering if he hadn't found a whole new future, with a whole new person.

Just sometimes. Like when Gabriel gave him floury kisses in the kitchen, or climbed into his lap in the cuddle chair after a rough scene to calm Aled down, or sent him pictures of cats from his walk to work while Aled had already been in the office for three hours.

Sometimes it felt like the world had changed — but Aled knew it was only him.

And went he opened the kitchen drawer, the first day in April, to find an old brown envelope staring mournfully back at him, Aled realised that it was time to stop living in the past.

* * * *

He grunted as he came, shaking so hard that the car rocked, and snarled when Gabriel coughed and choked, unable to take it. As the shaking ebbed away, and the feeling leaked back into Aled's limbs, he tightened his grip on Gabriel's hair and swore breathlessly at him for the failure.

"Clean it up."

Gabriel's tongue was rough against Aled's over-sensitised skin and Aled groaned again at the soft laps and drags as Gabriel removed all evidence of his failure.

"You're going to have to practice."

"Yes, sir."

Aled pushed down on Gabriel's head. "Don't talk with your mouth full. Finish it."

Gabriel's breath was hot against him and he whimpered once before that tongue resumed its task. The denim would taste foul and he would want a drink after.

Aled had no intention of giving it to him.

When he was clean, Aled released the handful of hair that he'd used to force Gabriel's head down onto his cock and stroked it smooth. Gabriel rested his cheek against Aled's thigh and waited, licking his lips absently, and Aled smiled.

"Want more?"

"Yes, sir."

"You can do it again when I get back."

"Won't you want to fuck me proper when you get back, sir?"

Gabriel's tone was playful and Aled casually lifted a hand and slapped his bare arse. The crack was deafening and Gabriel cried out. Aled narrowed his eyes and did it again. This time, as a red handprint blossomed, Gabriel bit his lip, whining on Aled's lap like a newly broken-in sex slave.

Now *there* would be a game. Aled made a mental note.

"You keep quiet, or I'll put a gag between your teeth and you can find out what it's like to be filled at both ends."

"Yes, sir."

"You want me to fuck you properly, is that it?"

"Please, sir."

"Well, then. I'll tell you what. When I get back from my errand," Aled crooned, smoothing down Gabriel's hair, "you can have another try at sucking my dick. And if you do it right that time, I'll take you down a nice little alley you undoubtedly know and you can pick your favourite stretch of wall to be fucked against."

Gabriel shivered, licking his swollen lips. Aled hooked his finger into the metal collar hanging loose at his neck and jerked him back upright into the passenger seat.

"Now, I have a prior engagement for lunch," he said, padlocking the collar to the metal rods at the base of the headrest. "You stay here, nice and quiet and still, and I'll even give you a little something to entertain yourself. But you have to be good, or someone will see you."

Gabriel stiffened and Aled laughed, tracing his thumb over the blindfold.

"Trinity Walk car park," he said softly. "Just the blacked-out windows between you and a couple of hundred shoppers."

Gabriel's jaw sagged and Aled kissed the slack mouth. Slowly. Hungrily. *Promising.*

"So I'll leave you something to entertain yourself with," Aled said, opening the glovebox and taking out the vibrator he'd stashed for situations just like these. He slapped Gabriel's knees casually apart and thrust the device up into his cunt brutally hard, tutting when he whined and deliberately stroking his swollen cock as he switched the vibrator on. Gabriel's thighs clamped around his wrist, but Aled pulled free and patted his thigh. "If it comes out, I'll put it back and make sure it *can't* come out. Understood?"

"Y-yes, sir."

"Good." Aled leaned close and kissed him again, before whispering, "Colour?"

A ghost of a smile. "Green."

Aled patted his knee again, then tucked himself into his jeans, grabbed the folder off the dashboard and got out, locking the car behind him and heading for the lifts, the picture of cool composure, not attracting a second glance.

Leaving Gabriel in the car, stark naked but for the blindfold and collar and a vibrator torturing him with no release.

Aled idly reflected that Gabriel looked damn good in a blindfold and he'd have to use it more often, and stabbed the button for the ground floor. He felt antsy. Despite the blowjob, he felt too big for his own skin, too energetic, too—

Nervous.

And yet—

There was a kind of strange goodness about it. As though he were shaking something off, brushing away chains and cobwebs and rolling the weight off his shoulders.

The coffee shop was only across the road from the car park, not quite in the hustle and bustle of the city centre proper, and she was already there. Aled could see her auburn hair, glowing gently in the wintry sun, even from the pavement, and he ducked into the coffee shop with that nervous energy reaching a fever pitch, bubbling up out of his skin so much that when she stood and held out her hand, he ducked in to hug her, rather than shake it.

"Uh—"

"Sorry. Hi."

Melissa coloured faintly and nodded. "Hi." She sat gingerly, eyeing him, then her gaze dropped to the folder and she bit her lip.

"This is yours," Aled said, handing it over.

"And it's—"

"All signed," Aled said and her shoulders relaxed. "Your solicitor will have to get in touch with mine and we'll have to both contact the bank independently to close the holiday account down, but it's all signed."

"You—you're not going to contest any of it?"

"No."

Her shoulders sagged and a smile began to form.

"You're being more than fair. And I don't want to—I know I've dragged this out and I'm sorry. I wasn't ready to move on, wasn't ready to accept that I'd failed—"

Melissa shook her head. "We both failed."

Aled blinked.

"We changed, Aled," she said softly, squeezing his wrist over the table. It was the first time she'd touched him in over a year and her skin felt alien. It felt like a stranger's hand, despite all their years together and Aled exhaled.

There was no hum.

His skin had always buzzed and hummed when Melissa touched him, like an electric shock. And now there was nothing.

Aled — smiled.

"We just changed," she continued softly. "We wanted different things and in the end, one of us would have to have been miserable. And I do still love you. I'll always love you."

"You just love your future children more."

She smiled sadly. "Does that make me a bad person?"

"No," Aled said honestly. "It's going to make you an amazing mum one day, though."

"I do hope you find someone else, Aled," she said, squeezing his wrist again. "I really do. I hated leaving you, I hated seeing you hurting with this — this paperwork..."

"I didn't want to admit I'd failed," Aled said, "and when I finally figured out that it was my failing at being married, my letting my dad down —"

"Oh, Aled, you never let him down —"

"—more than it was about *you*, about specifically *you*...does that make sense? I was gutted at losing my wife, at losing my marriage, but...not about losing *you*."

"It does," she admitted. "It was how I felt when I left. I realised I was hanging on to my marriage, not my Aled. And I knew I had to go before we started to hate each other. I never hated you, never wanted to hate you, never wanted you to hate me —"

"I don't."

She bit her lip. "Thank you."

"It'll always hurt, that we didn't work out," Aled said honestly, "but I'm moving on and I did a lot of soul-searching before I signed those papers, and you know what? I want you to be happy. I really do. I want you to settle down with some other man and have a whole football team of kids if you both want them, because I'll always love you, even if it's not the way I did when I married you, and you're going to make a brilliant mum."

She made a little noise, her eyes shining, then suddenly stood up, came around the table and hugged him.

Hard.

Aled breathed in her smell — the familiar perfume, the faint underlay of hospital disinfectant, the barely-there scent of her favourite shampoo — and closed his eyes. His heart ached, but it didn't *hurt* the way it had before. He loved her and he'd always love her but —

But he no longer looked at Melissa the way he'd found himself looking at Gabriel.

"Find someone," Melissa whispered, squeezing him tight. "Find someone who fits around all your little edges and tells you you're being a tit when you are, and cuddles you when you need one, and *knows* you. Someone who loves you, every last bit of you, and who makes you every bit as good as you could be. You deserve someone like that."

Aled nodded, letting go. "I think…maybe I have. Just have to work on keeping them, now."

Melissa smiled and sank slowly back into her seat. "Stay?" she asked. "For lunch? Let's just…have lunch, and talk, and part ways well. Instead of that horrible silence after I walked out and having arguments in public by your car."

"Hey, *you* started those."

"And you joined in. Don't give me that crap," she sniped, then her face softened and she propped her chin on her hand. "Are you in love again?"

Aled frowned, thinking of the naked man in his car — the man with the bedroom eyes, the man who danced while he played pool, the man who hated science fiction yet watched it religiously out of sheer horror, the man who threw flour on him, the man who grumbled about octopuses in the middle of a good cuddle, the man who was shy about triggers but would walk around a stranger's house in nothing but a T-shirt, the man who begged to be fucked but then quieted and curled into a hug like he didn't quite know how to ask for those —

"You know what? Maybe I am."

Want to see more from this author?
Here's a taster for you to enjoy!

Starting Over: The Other Man
Matthew J. Metzger

Excerpt

Gabriel didn't stir when Aled removed the collar.

He was a mess. A ridiculously beautiful, tempting mess. The collar had left a thin red line on his alabaster skin, framed by the bruises either side where Aled had bitten him. His legs were in a similar state, especially his inner thighs. Aled liked Gabriel's inner thighs, and it showed. One wrist was a little swollen from all the twisting around he'd done on their first day, and Aled made a mental note to check it again once they were home.

He ghosted his fingers over the raised skin and squeezed.

Nothing.

"Unbelievable," he muttered and shook Gabriel by the shoulder. "Come on, Gabe. We need to go."

Gabriel hated that nickname. Usually it earned Aled the mother of all scowls. But this time? Nothing.

"Gabe."

A low grumble emanated from the inert lump, and it became even more lumplike—the hand in Aled's slid free, seized the duvet and pulled. In a heartbeat, Gabriel was buried in the rumpled remains of the bed and not an inch of skin could be seen.

"I guess age really is just a number."

Aled wanted to leave him to it, but it was quarter to eleven and they only had fifteen minutes to check out and return the keys. And *he* was ready to go. Their bags were by the door, tidily packed. Every surface was clean. He'd even done the last sweep of the bathroom to check for abandoned soap or forgotten aftershave. The only thing left was to pour Gabriel into a T-shirt and jeans and stuff him in the car.

Which — from a lot of experience — Aled knew was easier said than done.

It wasn't that difficult if Gabriel was just asleep. Turfing him out of bed for work in the morning was easy enough. But after a game? No chance. And it had been a *long* game.

They'd met nearly two years ago after a random hook-up on Grindr. Aled had been going through a divorce, and Gabriel had been — still was — a sex fiend. They'd figured out pretty fast that Aled's dominant tendencies and Gabriel's sexual fantasies lined up neatly, and had been playing on a regular basis ever since. Hence the collar.

And hence the coma, because Gabriel after a whole weekend of being used and abused could sleep like the dead.

"All right," Aled said, turning up the bottom of the duvet. "You leave me no choice."

He found an ankle. The minute he wrapped his fingers around it, the leg was dragged away. But Aled was used to pinning down fighting bodies and simply pitted his weight against Gabriel's. And given Gabriel was a wiry little wretch and Aled was in his mid-thirties and growing an appropriately sized spare tyre around his gut, it was always going to go in his favour.

Dragging on the ankle produced a calf. At the other end of the calf lay the sensitive back of a knee. And above that, a thigh that Aled could seize in both hands and use like a lever. A moment later, he had an armful of squirming plaything, and he squeezed Gabriel to his chest in a bear hug before standing up and depositing that battered, naked body on the rug.

Then dark eyes were staring up at him from the vicinity of his crotch, and his brain short-circuited.

Maybe they could be a *little* la—

He shook himself. No. The cabin had been expensive enough. Paying for a whole extra day wasn't on the cards.

"If you're in that car in the next five minutes, I'll fuck you at the border," he offered.

"You won't."

Gabriel's voice was raspy and hoarse. He'd spent the better part of seventy-two hours either screaming, begging or gagged. His lips were still flushed and swollen and the breathy quality to his words was another unhelpful aphrodisiac.

Aled raised his eyebrows and straightened his spine. That cool edge of power started to flicker around the edges of his psyche once more.

"I will."

"You're chafing."

Aled winced. He *was* a bit raw. "Don't need my cock to count as a fuck."

"No deal."

He laughed, the mood dissipating. He knew that tone.

"All right, beautiful. But we do need to go. I'll buy you lunch at the border, how's that?"

That was apparently more agreeable. Gabriel pushed himself up on shaky limbs and reached for the clothes Aled had laid out.

Gabriel's twenty-sixth birthday had been at the weekend and Aled's present had been a long, *long* sex game. They were both kinky, despite Aled's bland ginger-with-glasses, chubby-thirties and job-in-marketing appearance. Aled wasn't always entirely *comfortable* with his sexual preferences — who got off on rape fantasies, after all? — but Gabriel had no such room for doubts. He liked nothing more than to be dragged down fighting and fucked raw.

So that was what Aled had done. From Friday afternoon right through to Monday morning.

He'd 'kidnapped' Gabriel from work and driven him up to this lonely, snow-covered cabin in the Scottish Highlands. It was intended for hikers, but they'd never left. In the midst of a dark forest, miles from civilisation and buried under three and a half feet of snow, he had treated Gabriel like a sex slave — and there hadn't been a whisper of a safeword the entire time.

Basically, he'd fucked Gabriel stupid for his birthday.

"Come on," he coaxed, when he'd come back from putting the bags in the car and found Gabriel still shirtless. "We need to go."

"Don't want to go."

Aled laughed. "You sound like a petulant kid."

"I'm on holiday!"

"We have to check out at eleven. Tell you what," Aled added when Gabriel scowled. "We'll stop for a massive pub lunch at the border, and I'll blow you in the toilets after if you're good and don't flirt with half the country on the way down."

Gabriel grumbled but tilted his head back against Aled's shoulder. Aled obediently kissed his ear.

That had been the basis of the game. They had an open relationship by mutual agreement—Gabriel regularly slept with other men, and had full-blown relationships with at least one of them. Aled had the same option in theory, but so far hadn't indulged. It worked, and worked well. But some of Aled's favourite games were when he pretended it was a problem. So, the kidnap had been on the premise that he was sick of Gabriel's playing away. He'd spent the weekend reminding Gabriel who he belonged to.

Supposedly. The truth was somewhere in the middle. Aled *didn't* mind the playing away. He even liked it sometimes, for the way he could exploit it for their own games—and not having to do bloodplay. But—

Lately, he'd found himself getting tired of driving Gabriel home after their scenes. Of booking taxis to and from the flat and the house. Of having to make sure they left enough time at the end of an evening to go their separate ways.

Aled didn't *want* to go their separate ways anymore.

But Gabriel was still a wild thing. Completely undomesticated. Aled was sure he'd baulk at the idea of living together and run a mile. So Aled hadn't said anything. What they had was great. Why risk it for the sake of an extra cuddle in the morning? So Aled kissed Gabriel's ear again and let go, smacking his arse to propel him towards the door. He wanted more—but it wasn't worth risking everything over.

"Can I have my phone back?" Gabriel asked as he wriggled into a bra and T-shirt, inky black hair sticking up all over the place in an impressive bedhead.

Aled raised an eyebrow sardonically. "Excuse me?"

Gabriel paused then dropped his gaze. "Please can I have my phone back, sir?"

"Why."

It wasn't a question—it was a demand.

"To—to check my messages, sir—"

"Has someone been messaging you?"

"I don't know."

"I haven't been messaging you. Who else could be?"

"Nobody important, sir."

"Damn right," Aled drawled. "And if it's nobody important, then you don't need to see it. Do you?"

"No, sir."

"Then I think I'll keep hold of it a while longer."

Gabriel swallowed, but nodded. "Yes, sir."

"Go out to the car, then. And no more arguing."

He was too raw for another fuck, or even a blow job. But after the hint of more playing, his libido was interested again. So once he'd locked up, he turned on Gabriel at the car and shoved him up against the boot, pressing his chest into the cold glass of the rear windscreen.

"Drop 'em and bend over."

"Sir?"

"*Now.*"

Gabriel fumbled with his jeans. "Please don't," he said and Aled heard the veiled warning. "It'll hurt—"

"I'm not going to fuck you," he said calmly, drawing the toy from his coat pocket. "I'd fall asleep at the wheel. But you obviously need a bit more practice with your lessons."

The plug was small, Aled's concession to Gabriel's soreness, but he pushed it in relentlessly and dry, forcing Gabriel still with a hand on his hip, until it was buried to the base. Gabriel whined, and Aled kissed his neck as he pulled the jeans back up and zipped Gabriel back in.

"Get fussy on the way home, and I'll switch it on."

Gabriel shuddered, and Aled backed up. He slapped his arse again, hard, and Gabriel near-yowled.

"Get in the car. Your phone's in the glovebox. On flight mode. You keep it that way—you can play your stupid games, but you don't put it on the network and start playing away again, got it?"

"Yes, sir."

Aled turned him, fisted a hand in Gabriel's hair and kissed him properly. He could still taste sex and salt on Gabriel's tongue. It was a heady combination, but it was also too soon for anything more.

Aled drew off and shoved. "Go."

Gabriel went.

PUBLISHING

Sign up for our newsletter and find out about all our romance book releases, eBook sales and promotions, sneak peeks and FREE romance books!

About the Author

Matthew J. Metzger is an asexual, transgender British author juggling books, an office job and a love of travel with the human need for sleep once in a while. He writes both adult and young adult books focusing on LGBT+ characters and their relationships, particularly those from the less salubrious areas in which he was dragged up over the years.

On the very rare occasions that Matt isn't writing, he can usually be found at the gym, halfway up a mountain or collecting new tattoos. (And yes, he does have book ink...)

Matthew loves to hear from readers. You can find his contact information, website details and author profile page at https://www.pride-publishing.com